# DEXTER CHASE

# FULL

## Gay Disclosure

### NAUGHTY COLLEGE MEN

**About the Publisher**

**4Fun Publishing,** a member of **BLVNP Incorporated**, 340 S. Lemon #6200, Walnut CA 91789, info@blvnp.com / legal@blvnp.com
NOTE: Due to the highly emotional reaction of some people to works of erotic fiction, any email sent to the above address that contains foul language or religious references is automatically deleted by our anti-spam software and will not be seen. All other communications are welcome.

**DISCLAIMER**
Please don't be stupid and kill yourself. This book is a work of FICTION. Do not try any new sexual practice that you find in this book. It is fiction and not to be confused with reality. Neither the author nor the publisher or its associates assume any responsibility for any loss, injury, death or legal consequences resulting from acting on the contents in this book. Every character in this book is over 18 years of age. The author's opinions are not to be construed as the opinions of the publisher. The material in this book is for entertainment purposes ONLY. Enjoy.

# Full Gay Disclosure

## Naughty College Men

By: Dexter Chase

© Dexter Chase 2015

ISBN: 978-1-68030-284-4

# Chapter 1

The dean walked into the staff common room looking very smug, accompanied by what all the staff members guessed to be a new staff member. They checked him out; he was an even, six footer, built like an American Football player, impressive. The staff realized straightaway that something momentous was going to be announced. For a long time, the dean had walked around with a beaten look. Not surprising really, school discipline had gone to the dogs and it had overflowed onto the college campus. Successive governments made it impossible to punish students transmitting itself to anarchy in the lecture rooms. Lecturers had virtually ceased to try teaching and usually sat reading or processing further qualifications while the students did whatever they wanted. They came to college mainly because that was a good place to meet all their friends and it was warm and dry, and most importantly kept them out of the workplace. Tom Howard spent more time interviewing new staff and appointing new dorm supervisors than he did in actioning the education department's directives.

"Ladies and gentlemen, good morning."

They all chorused the reply and Tom, grinning like an idiot continued, "I would like to introduce to you the new CDO and that stands for *College Disciplinary Officer*. Jarek Howard is my younger brother so this appointment gives me double pleasure. The government has at last acted on the discipline problem and they have chosen us to try the new program. All and I mean all restrictions on punishment are lifted. Jarek will be able to do anything he likes to students sent to him for punishment. If a student refuses to accept the punishment, Jarek will refer him to me and the student will be sent down and incarcerated in the first of the junior prisons. It is where discipline will be enforced by men whom we have called *goons* in a previous regime. A female CDO is currently in training and will be with us within the next month."

Tom went on describing how the system would work in practice.

"I am appointing a new batch of dorm supervisors from the two senior years and Jarek will always have two with him to witness punishment and if he wishes they can take part. Most punishment will take place in the CDO's room but if he considers it beneficial, he may interrupt a lecture and conduct the punishment in the lecture room of the student concerned. I will be making announcements during the assembly tomorrow morning. I'll be posting notices on all college boards. I am also going to introduce a uniform code which again will be strictly enforced."

There were gasps at that since no one had ever tried to put college students in uniform.

"Please, try not to send him too many students at once, just the worst cases. I'm sure that the numbers will very quickly drop to near zero because Jarek has told me what he intends to do. No student, however bold, will want to see him twice and I understand the female CDO will be equally as awful. I will leave Jarek with you for an hour and then he will spend the remainder of today briefing our new supervisors."

The staff bombarded Jarek with questions and at the end of the hour could hardly wait to get to their classrooms for the last day of anarchy. Jarek took over the double room allocated to him and was soon sitting with twelve boys who were the dean's original appointees but who had resigned because they considered it impossible to do their job.

"I am going to make this easy for you. I know you are all serious students who excel in sports and academics, so asking you to witness some of the actions I am going to take may not appeal to you. I am going to tell you now and it is no shame if you want to leave. I am allowed to cane bad boys, but I am going to make most of my punishments embarrassing and humiliating. That means the student will be made to strip and depending on his attitude and crime, will be made to carry out degrading sexual acts. Nothing is forbidden so I be the complete sadist and even use anal intercourse as a punishment. I will, on convenient occasions, use you boys to render the punishment. Of course, you will only be delivering it not receiving it. Now, if any of you thinks you won't be able to handle that you may leave."

No one moved.

"Good. Now first thing's first, from now on nothing you see or hear concerning my job is ever discussed with other people. If you betray that trust you will receive my worst punishment."

Still, no one moved.

"Alright, I want you all to strip naked and then get an erection."

There were gasps and looks of shock on all of their faces, but there were ten naked boys all playing with themselves within minutes and two headed for the door in double quick time. Jarek was impressed. He had read the Kinsey report years ago and every one of his ten were above average in cock size for their age and ethnicity.

"Well done, boys, you may now get dressed and sit down. I did that because I don't want any little coy boys when the crunch comes to administer discipline. I'll now go into detail on how this is going to work. I want all of your lecture rosters so that I can use you without disrupting your studies too much."

The more Jarek spoke, the more shocked and enthusiastic the boys became. By the time he finished he had to remind them, "Under no circumstances are you to discuss this outside of these rooms."

They all confirmed their understanding and left with a million words they wanted to spout to each other. Many of those were said in the outer office and Jarek listened with a broad grin on his face. His guess was that he would have no problems with these ten young men.

Jarek then set about organizing his domain. All sessions would be secretly filmed by two hidden cameras that had already been wired in and would be activated by a switch at Jarek's desk. Besides his desk and chair, in this room there were two other chairs, a table, and a punishment bench, a rack contained canes and there was a box, eighteen inches high, wide enough and long enough for two boys to stand on it together, placed six feet in front of Jarek's desk. It was a neat platform to emphasize to the punishment candidates their position. There was a bathroom off this room, a door that led to another room, and the exit. The outer room contained four chairs bolted to the floor and on the arms were wrist restraints to be used for offenders waiting to be punished. In one corner of the main room was a filing cabinet where records would be kept including DVDs of the punishment sessions. Jarek had the only key to it.

College security would be used to transfer bad boys from their lectures to the outer office.

Jarek was lodging with his brother until he could find an apartment so it was easy to fill Tom in on what he had done with his day.

"If this experiment works, Jarek, you could end up with a very good career in this new environment. At only 25 you are well placed to take advantage of it."

Jarek grinned, "Mmm, should keep me happy for years."

Tom laughed because he knew his brother was gay.

"Just remember that you can only be a voyeur on this one, no touchy feely."

Still grinning, Jarek replied, "I know but I think I can handle that."

Tom had looked after Jarek after their parents died and was almost like a father to him because of their age difference. But they had always got on well and he hoped that would continue.

The next morning, during the students' general assembly, the dean informed them of the situation.

"Many of you came here for a free ride for three years and those who came to study have suffered for it. Starting today, that will all change. Those of you who don't want to pursue their studies are free to leave. If you remain, you will be subjected to the most severe punishment if you misbehave. The new law becomes effective immediately. If you remain and misbehave, you will accept the new College Disciplinary Officer's punishment or you will be taken away and incarcerated in one of the new junior prisons, where the disciplinary routine will be even more severe and you will suffer a loss of freedom for not less than one year."

There were hoots of derision but most of them lacked enthusiasm.

"Assembly is dismissed and those of you who are leaving are to do so by lunchtime, after that the new rules will apply. Remember, there are no limits to the CDO's punishments and the alternative is prison. A female CDO will be in place within the next month with the same remit. Let me also remind you that punishment will not necessarily be conducted in the privacy of the CDO's rooms."

Jarek sat back in his office after the assembly and started setting up his computer with the necessary apps to make his job easy when it came time to review records of repeat offenders and to reference individual student stats. He also started devising his punishments for different offences. His training had given him the broad outline, it was now up to him how he handled it and his future would depend on its success.

The first lectures had only been progressing for about half an hour after lunch when he got his first call from a young female lecturer that had taken verbal abuse from a student who didn't believe the dean. He swaggered into Jarek's outer office a few minutes later between two security guards, not that his size dictated that, and was shocked when he sat down and Jarek had him secured to a chair.

"You can remain there, Mr. Chambers, until my two supervisors arrive and Professor Harkins finishes her lecture."

Peter Chambers was most uncomfortable with this quick action and began to wonder if he had made a mistake. He continued to dig a hole for himself by shouting at Jarek through the door where the latter had gone, back to his main room.

End of lecture and Peter squirmed as two seniors entered, looked at him disdainfully before going to Jarek's office and closing the door. A few minutes later, Janet Harkins joined them. She was a young assistant professor, the same age as Jarek, very petite and pretty.

Jarek offered Janet a chair next to his own and the two seniors stood at the side of the desk, already briefed by Jarek. Justin and Daniel were looking a little apprehensive as Jarek told them what was going to happen. Janet's eyes got wider as he progressed, and then she laughed.

"I'm sorry, Jarek. But I can't see you getting Chambers to do that."

"Oh, he'll do it because the alternative is prison."

After completing his briefing, Jarek went to the outer office, locked the exit door, and removed the wrist restraint from a very much quieter student.

"Follow me, Chambers."

Peter had no choice really so he did.

"Stand up on the raised platform and face my desk."

Peter stood there, feeling a little less sure of himself than he previously had.

"Now, Chambers listen carefully because your choices are very limited. You will answer truthfully every question I ask you. If you lie and I find out, you go to prison. You do everything I tell you to do or you go to prison. There are no other alternatives. The only leeway you have is that if you refuse an order but then reconsider before I summon security to take you away I will increase your punishment. In other words, the more co-operative you are the milder the punishment. Do you understand?"

"Yeah, what's not to understand?"

"And you will address everyone in this room as 'Sir' or 'Ma'am.' Now, remove your shoes and socks."

Peter looked at the CDO as though he was mad, until Jarek snarled at him, "Now!"

Looking a little bemused, Peter did as he was told.

"Next, your sweater and T-shirt, now!"

Peter was quite proud of his body so he did, striking a pose when he was done.

The torso was lightly muscled but extremely attractive. All of his muscles were clearly defined but looked natural.

*'This is a student that doesn't spend much time in a gym but has been lucky enough to be gifted with a very attractive torso,'* was Jarek's thought. He also still looked like a school boy so Jarek checked details on his computer. The boy was a freshman so he would be eighteen or nineteen. Jarek's file showed that Peter had celebrated his nineteenth birthday half-way through his first term.

"Very nice, Mr. Chambers, now Justin and Daniel, remove his trousers."

Peter looked shocked and then voiced his dissent, "No fucking way."

"That is one extra punishment and if the trousers are not on the floor without further protest, you will be on your way to prison."

Jarek picked up his phone as he spoke and Peter looked worried. He quickly allowed the two supervisors to unclip the top of his jeans and pull the zip down. The trousers fell to the floor and he kicked them off. He stood straight, blushing, and covering the front of his groin with his hands, looking at Janet. The white briefs gave Jarek a twinge in his groin. He realized that Peter Chambers was a very sexy young man.

"Very nice, Mr. Chambers, rotate 360 degrees so that we can see all of you, well almost all of you."

Peter did, slowly, and Jarek had an expanding lump in his trousers. *'The cute butt would look very good impaled on his cock,'* was Jarek's thought.

*'God, the boy is stunning.'*

"Very nice, Peter, now Justin and Daniel remove his briefs and let Professor Harkins see if he is a real man."

Peter just shook his head. He was in shock as he tried to hold onto his briefs.

"I will add another punishment if those briefs haven't joined your trousers by the time I count to five."

Jarek got to two. Once again, Peter covered his groin with his hands.

"Put your hands by your sides, face the professor, and apologize for your behavior. I want to hear the sincerity in that apology."

Peter was not feeling quite so smug now and cast a sidelong glance at the two seniors who made his embarrassment worse because both of them were staring at his groin. Jarek had briefed them to do that.

Sounding very unsure of himself, Peter apologized adequately to Janet.

"If you had obeyed me from the start your punishment would have ended there. Since you were delayed in following orders, your final punishment will be to get an erection and show us how much of a man you are."

There were gasps of shock from everyone else.

"If you balk at this, the next punishment will be much worse."

Peter wanted to cry. This was so humiliating he just shook his head.

"Very well," Jarek said and picked up his phone again.

Peter started to play but took a very long time to get an erection. When it was complete, Jarek was almost drooling. The boy was only medium height but his cock was way above average in length, circumcised, and gorgeous with a nice set of balls beneath.

"Your final punishment, if you obey immediately, is to jack off and orgasm into your hand."

Peter looked at Jarek, saw the expression on his face, and started to masturbate. Janet was fascinated, the two seniors were intrigued, and

Jarek's erection hurt. Peter couldn't remember ever taking this long to cum. He did eventually, catching his discharge in his hand.

"Well done, Peter. You may go to the bathroom," Jarek said, pointing to the door, "And clean up."

Turning to the others Jarek spoke, "You may all go now. Janet, I hope you think the punishment was adequate."

They both laughed and Jarek finished, "Remember, this must not be discussed outside of this office, ever."

They left while Jarek waited for Peter to return. Pointing to the raised platform again, Jarek told him, "Stand there and face me, legs astride, hands behind your back."

"Peter, you are a stunning young man. I am sure by your looks that you are also a very popular one. Your stats show that even though you are a royal pain in the arse to your lecturers you return good results. I now want you to use your assets to help return lecture rooms into serious places of learning. If I see you in this room again for punishment, you will be extremely sorry because this session was as mild as you will ever see. I have unlimited powers to humiliate and embarrass you, remember that."

Peter nodded but was still too embarrassed to speak. Jarek walked round his desk and put out his hand.

"No hard feelings on my part."

Peter looked at the hand and then took it. He could also see the bulge where Jarek was still partly erect. He looked up into Jarek's face and was immediately flustered. He wasn't sure what he saw in the eyes, but it certainly wasn't what he expected.

"No, Sir," came out a little strangled.

"I'm pleased. You can get dressed now and leave."

Peter was way off-balance walking to his next lecture. *'What was that look on the CDO's face as we shook hands?'* was his thought.

Jarek sat back and thought about this first session. It had gone well but he was disturbed at how turned on he had been by Peter Chambers. *'I can legally have an affair with him if he is gay. I must ask Tom what the college rules are regarding liaisons between staff and students.'* That thought kept recurring as he went through this first day.

Jarek had two more similar cases to deal with on that first day, neither of them exciting him at all and neither of them going any further than he had with Peter. He did, however, have an interesting one to carry over to the next day. Two second year students had thrown punches in the middle of a lecture. He would think about their punishment and make sure that his two witnesses had some fun as well.

# Chapter 2

That night after his sister-in-law had retired, Jarek brought up the subject of student-staff relationships.

"Tom, does the college have a policy on students and staff being in relationships?"

Tom looked hard at his brother before replying, "This is 2050, Jarek, we are much more liberal than of old. The rules are reasonably simple. We conform to civil law so all of our students being over eighteen can have relationships with staff members. The only restriction is that you cannot have a lover who is in your lecture classes. In your case, with no lecture classes, you can sleep with the whole student body if you wish, and of course all of the staff."

Tom laughed then before continuing, "Academic interest or personal?"

Jarek blushed a little, "Oh, academic."

Tom was too knowledgeable about human nature, and his brother, to accept that so he just said, "Be careful, Jarek. I wouldn't want to see you hurt or in trouble."

Jarek knew and moved across the room to hug his brother.

"Thanks, Dad. I'll behave."

The brothers laughed together as they headed for bed.

Jarek slept badly, Peter Chambers kept impinging on his thoughts.

Feeling jaded and unfocussed, Jarek went through the first punishment session on automatic. The two students who fought were made to undress each other, an article at a time. It was so embarrassing that it required several threats from Jarek for them to comply. Once they were naked, he made the most truculent one get on his knees in front of the other and play with him. Only after much protesting did he comply.

"You are making things very much worse for yourself, Andrews. I can keep racking up the punishment for a lot longer if you won't comply with my orders. When Smith is erect you are to kiss the end of his penis and tell it how much you love its size. Failure to comply instantly and I promise you will be swallowing it all."

More dissent so Jarek talked him through the final punishment provided he complied.

"Listen very carefully, Andrews, because your whole future hinges on you understanding the next two orders without further dissent. The third order if I have to give it will, I am sure please my two witnesses because they will be given permission to bugger you, and you will have no choice in the matter because you will be restrained."

"Now, use your mouth and tongue to pleasure Smith's cock and balls. I want to see real enthusiasm and that enthusiasm should be more than sufficient to make him cum in less than fifteen minutes or you get buggered. When he cums, you swallow it all and lick his deflating cock clean."

The look of shock was enough to make Jarek smile, and the session finished with Andrews swallowing a mouthful of cum. Smith on the other hand hoped he could instigate another fight where he could be construed as the innocent party. A blowjob was a new and exciting experience for him.

Both offenders dressed and Jarek addressed them, "Smith, you have seen some of the things I am capable of and you have the sense to do as you were told. Andrews, you're an idiot. You could have got off the same as Smith. If you ever come back here, we will start where you left off today. Now back to your lectures."

Jarek noticed both witnesses had gotten erections watching it and one of them could not hide the fact that he had cum in his trousers. Jarek made him stay behind.

"Marcus, I had no intentions of embarrassing you in front of your colleague but I think you are gay and just wanted confirmation."

Marcus blushed and tried not to look at Jarek as he mumbled, "Whatever gave you that preposterous idea?"

Jarek grinned and told him to look at the front of his trousers. Marcus almost fainted with embarrassment.

"Oh fuck, I'm sorry, Sir. It was just so sexually arousing."

Jarek laughed, "Yes, I know, that's why I wrapped mine in tissues to absorb the mess."

Marcus grinned then. "Yes, Sir, I'm gay. You won't let that interfere with my continued presence, will you?"

Jarek's reply made him even happier.

"Of course, it won't. I will even turn you loose on some of the recalcitrant students knowing that you'll enjoy it."

Jarek had just made a new friend.

Two more single punishments that were quite boring as there was little dissent so it never got past jacking-off in front of his two witnesses.

During a lull in activity, Jarek pulled up every fact he could about Peter Chambers before calling Marcus for a quick chat in between lectures.

"Do you know Peter Chambers, Marcus?"

"Only vaguely, Sir, we have no lectures together because he's a freshman."

"Strictly between you and me, I would like you to try to find out if he is gay."

Marcus wasn't stupid. 'The CDO fancies Chambers,' was his immediate thought.

Close observation of Peter over several days gave Marcus the idea that he probably was gay, or at least was interested in other guys' groin areas. A casual chat with Peter, an invitation to join him for a swim and Marcus was sure enough to tell Jarek.

"I think there is a very good chance that he is, Sir. He certainly shows a lot of interest in other guys' groins."

Jarek engineered it that he would pass the lecture room where Peter was in as his last lecture of the day, and made sure to bump into him.

"Oh, hello Chambers, how are you doing?"

Peter was a little flustered because he had thought a lot about this new man.

Rather tentatively, Peter replied, "I'm doing ok, Sir."

"Good, if you haven't anything else on for a while I wondered if you would like to come to my office for a chat with me."

Peter looked a little apprehensive.

"It's alright. You are definitely not in trouble."

They settled into Jarek's room with drinks from his fridge and Jarek started, "I just wanted to quiz you about the college. Please relax, but if you would be more comfortable standing on the platform naked, I won't complain."

Peter looked a little shocked, but at the same time his brain was working and he was feeling bold enough to make a suggestion.

"I don't mind, Sir, but as I'm not being punished I would only do it if you did the same."

Jarek couldn't believe his luck. He got up, locked the door and returned, but to the platform.

"Ok, join me. We'll match each other article for article."

Peter was a little hesitant so that it was Jarek who was naked first, but only by a few seconds. Looking at each other's groins, Jarek spoke first, "I think we have answered each other's question."

Peter nodded. He didn't know what to say. To him, Jarek was gorgeous.

Scoping him out, Peter realized that Jarek's body was like his own, only bigger. Lightly muscled but perfectly defined with a head of unruly, brownie silver hair, an unusual color for someone so young. He had laughing eyes and at the other end a good length, thick, circumcised cock. Peter didn't drool but he loved what he saw. He was longer than Jarek, but he only thought in terms of taking that cock in his arse, not the reverse.

"I should be moving into my own apartment in a couple of weeks' time. Provided you keep your nose clean, I would love you to be my first guest."

Peter tried not to gush.

"You can count on it."

Jarek moved in close and took Peter's face in his hands before moving closer and planting a soft kiss on his lips.

"I would like to do much more with you here, but I want it to be special and comfortable so we have to wait."

Peter nodded, "Ok, Sir, that's going to be hard now that I know, but I'll try."

Jarek laughed and continued, "You can drop the 'Sir' now as well, except when we are in our official capacities."

No problem and the two young men went their separate ways full of anticipation of something special taking place very soon.

The next student for punishment had verbally attacked a female student. Jarek thought about making him take his punishment in class, but decided he was too new at this to be sure of controlling it. Instead he talked to Marcus.

"Marcus, I have Shelley for punishment today and I was thinking of making him give you a blowjob. I don't want to embarrass you so who would you like as the second witness?"

"I think Jack Hudson may be gay as well, Jarek, so he would be a good partner."

Jarek checked rosters and called Hudson and Marcus for an after-lunch session with the punishment candidate.

Standing on the platform was a boy who would leave the CDO's room a much chastened figure later.

Jarek gave his brief, emphasizing the business of honest answers to questions.

"How often do you masturbate, Matthews?"

Paul Matthews looked shocked and then brazen.

"Not very often, Sir, I leave it to girls to satisfy me."

"Good to hear. How many blowjobs have you had in the last term?"

The boy blushed a little but brazened it out, "Too many to remember, Sir."

"So you're saying that you are something of an expert on blowjobs."

"Yeah, I guess," was the cocky reply.

"Very good, now I would like you to strip completely, ready for punishment."

Threats were required, but the end result was as required.

"I calculate that your initial refusals have added three more punishments. The first one is you playing with yourself and getting an erection."

Job done without a problem and Jarek could see why. The boy had the biggest cock he had ever seen.

*'God, if I had a cock that big, I would take every opportunity to show it off. It's huge.'*

Jarek looked at his two witnesses and noted both were trying to hide increased bulges in their trousers.

"Marcus and Jack, there is no need to be embarrassed. Paul has a truly impressive appendage. Why don't you let him undress you both and get your erections visible for comparison?"

Paul loved it. He had Marcus and Jack naked and erect in front of him. Neither of them had anything to be ashamed of. In fact, Jarek thought they were edible. Marcus was a slim, non-athletic sought, but he was sporting about nine inches. Jack was a vision, a Greek god, blonde, and gorgeous but with a cock only a little bigger than average for a white, Caucasian.

"Well, now that we have seen two more cocks for comparison, you can get down on your knees in front of Marcus, Paul, and show him how much your girlfriends have taught you. Blow him to orgasm. Any dissent and there is only one other orifice I can let them use."

Paul wasn't stupid.

"You can't do that. Buggery is way beyond the pale."

"You are correct, it is, but I am allowed to do anything I like including that. Now, blow Marcus and let me know what his cum tastes like."

Paul was gutted and gave Marcus a lousy blowjob.

Jarek then addressed Marcus, "If Jack would like one as well, you might like to teach Paul how to make it a good one as he didn't do a very good job with you."

Marcus would have kissed Jarek for this opportunity and Jack wasn't looking too upset either. Sitting comfortably with his legs spread wide, Jack was transported to heaven as Marcus made Paul slather his balls as well as stroke his torso and play with his nipples while exciting his cock. When he came, it was quite apparent that Jack had enjoyed a mighty orgasm because Paul had to let some of it escape his mouth.

After all had cleaned up, got dressed, and were back in position, Jarek spoke to Paul, "I will expect to hear within the next few days that you have made a very sincere apology to the girl you abused, otherwise I will invite her for a second session with you that will go further than today, if you get my meaning."

Paul understood completely and scuttled away very quickly when released.

"Jack, I presume you were not too unhappy with that?"

"Crikey no, Sir, I can accept any number of those."

"Good, now both of you. If I do take the next step with a bad boy would you be willing to take part in a little anal intercourse?"

Jack blushed almost scarlet, looking between Marcus and Jarek before stuttering out, "Would I bloody ever?"

Jarek couldn't disguise a smile but still managed to get out a reply to that.

"You used a profanity, and you know that is punishable. As your supervisor, I think I should make you give Marcus a blowjob."

Jarek read it correctly. Jack wanted to do it but tried not to look as if he did. Eventually, Jarek laughed.

"Alright Jack, I won't ask you to do it here. I'll leave you and Marcus to sort it out and if you go ahead you can do it in private." He emphasized the 'if' to make it clear he wasn't serious.

Both boys replied in unison as they looked at each other, "Thanks very much, Sir."

Too much, Jarek almost fell off his chair laughing and the two boys joined him.

"Well done and thank you for today."

Jarek was very happy with these two seniors. They were gorgeous and gay. The DVDs he recorded would be a constant source of pleasure to him in private and he knew he could use the two for the more extreme punishments.

During the day he used four of the other supervisors but only as witnesses and in one case as assistants in stripping a student.

Tom was delighted after conversing with lecturers at the end of the first week. Jarek's punishment sessions were having a dramatic effect because lecturers were sending him the ringleaders who became pussy cats after a session with Jarek.

The effectiveness of his actions left Jarek with a lot of free time which he used to refine the punishments. All of his ideas were committed to computer, ready for the day he hoped to be heading up the CDO program nationally. Looking further forward, he would instigate the program to schools as well. He would have to be a little less aggressive there, he thought, because the students would mainly be under eighteen, although sixteen was the legal age for sex. *'Different punishment regimes for under sixteen and sixteen to eighteen,'* he thought.

By the end of his first month, Jarek felt secure enough in his ability to use two boys in a public punishment session. They had been verbally quite disgusting during a biology lesson where the human body was being discussed. It resulted in a lecturer being scandalized and phoning Jarek. He thought before replying. Looked at his watch and realized he had more than half an hour of the lecture time left.

"I'll come to you for this one if you will allow me the remainder of the lecture period to humiliate the boys."

The professor had heard rumors about the goings on in the CDO's office and readily agreed.

Jarek entered the lecture room and picked out the two offenders. They were made to stand apart from everyone else. The other boys in the class had all heard what the CDO could do and did despite the *not telling* order so they were pleased they weren't the ones to be punished. The girls were looking at the two bad boys with smug expressions on their faces.

"These two are Lucas Adams and Jason Collins. They are both over eighteen, Mr. Howard, so there are no restrictions on their punishment."

"Thank you, Professor."

Jarek wondered how any student could offend against this one. She looked formidable.

"Collins and Adams, I will remind you of the rules. You will obey any order given to you by me, immediately. I will not tolerate any dissent because verbal abuse of a female teacher by a male student is totally unacceptable. If you balk at any order, I will initially add another stratum of punishment. If you balk a second time, I will send for security and you will be allowed to cool your heels for one year in a secure establishment. Do you understand?"

The two boys nodded and resigned themselves to some serious humiliation.

"Now, both of you strip naked."

They did, very quickly covering their genitals as soon as their boxers came off.

Jarek pointed to two spots on the floor and told them to stand there.

"Now girls, as part of your lecture on human anatomy, the male genitals are discussed so why don't you examine the ones on these two. I would place particular emphasis on your findings about the male reproductive organ in an erect state."

Jarek didn't need to say any more. The girls made the two boys put their hands behind their backs and then pulled up chairs and started playing. Justin was the first one erect but he was not very impressive. Lucas was much more impressive even before he was completely erect. Both boys were monumentally embarrassed.

Jarek looked around the room at the remainder of the boys and quickly picked up the ones that were excited by the action. He didn't think all the erect cocks were attached to gay guys but it was obvious there were some raging hormones among them. He then studied Justin and Lucas more carefully. Justin was built very much like Peter but his groin area was not as interesting. He was a handsome lad and Jarek was surprised, looking at him, that he had been abusive. Lucas was different. He had curly hair and a mean set to his mouth. Jarek guessed he was the instigator and Justin just followed his lead.

Jarek allowed the girls to play for a little while so he could chat with the professor. He found out that his assumption was correct. He then told the girls that they should explore Lucas' other end. He was bent over a desk and one girl continued to play with his cock while another girl slid a finger into his arse. He tried to stand up until admonished by Jarek. The finger-fucking went on for a little while with different girls taking part until Lucas orgasmed.

"I think that dirty boy should be punished, girls. I haven't brought a cane but I'm sure your hands will do just as well if you rotate. I suggest ten hard ones would be appropriate."

By the time they finished, Lucas was howling and had a bottom that was glowing.

"Both of you gather up your clothes, but do not dress. Follow me."

Jarek winked at the girls, excused himself from the professor, and walked back to his office with two naked boys behind him. Both of them were blushing furiously and keeping close to Jarek, hoping no one would see them. From his desk drawer, Jarek produced a tube of soothing gel.

"Lucas, bend over the punishment bench and spread your legs."

The thoroughly beaten boy did, without protest.

"Justin, rub the gel into Lucas' cheeks. Coat a finger in some and put your finger into his anus and rub it in gently as well."

Jarek stood and watched, having carefully adjusted his cock so that it wouldn't show as he came erect. He was pleased to see Justin get hard again, indicating that he was excited by what he was doing. While Lucas got hard because Justin was hitting his prostate as he fingered him, giving him a double feeling of well-being as the gel took away the pain on his buttocks. A few minutes of that and Jarek told them to stand up and move to the platform.

"You are obviously excited so face each other and give each other an orgasm, either using your hands or your mouths."

The shocked looks were captured on camera and Jarek had many a laugh during the next year every time he looked at this particular DVD. They did as they were told having been completely broken by the humiliation in the lecture room. All cleaned up after they had orgasmed, Jarek told Lucas to dress.

"Justin had the easy ride in the lecture so he will remain and I'll even things up with him."

Lucas scuttled out leaving a very apprehensive Justin. Jarek joined him on the platform, moved in close and took the boy's face in his hands, making him look into his eyes.

"I am quite a good judge of character which is one of the reasons I have this job. I think you are a pretty special young man that has been led astray. I also think that you are gay, or at least bisexual. I want you to know that if as CDO I was allowed to get involved with a student in this room, I would like to make love to you. Please don't make me punish you again, because that will upset me enormously."

Jarek then moved closer and just touched his lips to Justin's before releasing him.

"Get dressed and in your next biology lesson, apologize to your professor and the girls that you verbally abused."

Justin was reeling as he left. He hadn't thought seriously about his sexuality. He had played around with boys and girls at school but nothing serious. Now he thought about it and wondered how close Mr. Howard had come to the truth. Also, he now knew that the CDO was gay and that was information to store away.

# Chapter 3

Jarek had very carefully chosen the décor and fittings for his apartment. It was very masculine, but also warm and inviting. The carpets were deep blue throughout but each room's décor was different. The walls were clean fresh pastels. The wooden furniture had a lovely yellow hew and the soft furnishings were of vibrant colors. On the walls hung modernist prints, none of them framed. His bedroom contained a queen-sized bed and the predominant color was blue, ranging from the deep blue of the carpet to very pale sky blue on the walls. Lighting had been designed by an expert and could be varied according to the mood he wished to create. He had promised Peter Chambers that he would be his first guest and his planning worked round that.

Sitting at his desk the first morning after moving in, he felt that his apartment was as perfect as he could make it. He called Peter on his cell after the lectures.

"Hi Peter, this is Jarek Howard. How are you?"

Peter replied, rather breathlessly, "I'm fine, Sir. I thought you had forgotten me."

Sounding as serious as he felt he replied, "I couldn't do that. Hardly a day has passed since I met you that I haven't thought about you."

Peter hugged himself, this sounded so good.

"My apartment is now finished and I'm in residence. I promised you would be my first guest so I was wondering if you would like to come to dinner on Friday. I promise not to poison you with my cooking."

"Oh gosh, I'd love to. Just tell me the time and your address."

"I thought we might eat at about 8, but if you arrive at 7 we can chat and have a drink while I cook."

"That's fine, where?"

"Flat H, second floor of the Atlantic Building on Runaway Road, and the dress is casual, ok?"

"Ok, and I know it, Sir, I'll be there."

"Peter, I hope you will drop the 'Sir' when you arrive."

Peter laughed, "Ok, Jarek, I promise. See you Friday."

Jarek took particular care choosing the ingredients for dinner. He carried out all the preparations in such a way that he would appear very professional putting it all together while Peter watched. The apartment was already perfect so he went for a shower and a very close shave. He wore his briefest underwear and carefully tailored chinos that clung to his body in all the right places, topped off with a wasted polo. His hair was his only disappointment. It didn't matter what he did, it always looked unruly. Apart from that any discerning male or female would say he looked incredibly attractive.

Peter arrived on time, brandishing a bottle of wine tastefully wrapped. Jarek took the gift, pulled Peter to him, and kissed him softly on the lips.

"Welcome to my home, Peter. I'm so pleased to see you."

They walked through to the reception room and Peter was impressed. He could see the dining table set for two and the whole picture was very pleasing.

"You have a lovely apartment, Jarek. It felt so warm and welcoming as soon as I walked in."

Jarek was pleased. "It just mirrors what I feel about your presence."

He was surprised as he unwrapped the wine. It was a very decent, crisp, dry white Sancerre.

"I love the wine, Peter. I'll chill that and we can have that with the hors d'eouvres. In the meantime, what would you like to drink?"

The two of them had white wine and chatted happily about college and friends as Peter sat at the breakfast bar and watched Jarek cook.

"You put me to shame in the kitchen. Are you sure you didn't train as a chef?"

Jarek laughed with pleasure.

"No, honestly, I trained as a psychiatrist, but cooking has always been my hobby. My mother was a brilliant cook and I bugged her from about ten years old to teach me. You would be amazed how many friends I made at college after they had eaten with me once."

Lots of laughter and Peter replied, "Mmm, I can believe that. If it tastes as good as the preparation looks, I'll be your slave forever if I can eat here every day."

"That sounds like the best incentive I have ever had to make this meal extraordinarily good."

And it was. By the end of the meal, Peter would have killed for another like it.

"My God, Jarek, you've missed your calling. You should have become a chef not a CDO."

"Well, thank you kind Sir. But I couldn't do this for large numbers every day. It would kill my love for it. I will, however, cook for you every day if you are going to become my slave."

Peter searched Jarek's eyes and realized the look was what he had seen that first day.

"You mean it, don't you?"

Jarek nodded and looked embarrassed, "Yes, I don't want you as a slave, but I am as certain as I can be without touching you that I want you as my lover, my partner."

For Peter, that was a very heavy commitment and he wanted to step back a little from that one.

"That is too heavy for me, Jarek, but I would very much like to explore the possibility."

"Will you stay the night then?"

A beaming smile greeted that.

"Yes, please. But you have to promise to be gentle with me. I don't have a load of experience but I know what I want and what I like."

"I'm too impatient to take things slowly, so just stop me if I go too far or too fast."

"I doubt you'll go too far, but you could go too fast."

Nothing else needed to be said on that score. They sat nursing snifters of Cognac while finding out more about each other. Peter hadn't realized that the dean was Jarek's brother.

"I can believe he is your father because the age gap is pretty huge, isn't it, for you to be siblings?"

Jarek laughed with pleasure, remembering his mother's comment when he had brought up the same subject, "You were the biggest surprise of my life. We thought your brother was going to be an only child until he was 25 and I missed a period for the first time since I had him. You brought us nothing but joy though, since you arrived and your brother feels the same way."

Then he remembered the terrible day Tom came to his school to tell him that their parents had both been killed in a traffic accident. He was sixteen and from that day onwards, Tom had been father, mother, brother, and friend to him.

"He may be 25 years older than me but he is the best brother in the world. After our parents died, he became my mum, dad, brother, and friend, and still is."

Peter didn't delve any further. He guessed there was sorrow to be found there.

"Does he know you are gay?"

"Yes, I told him when he took over my caring. He has always been supportive, guiding me through the maze of my sexuality."

When the Cognac was finished, Jarek helped Peter to his feet. Took him in his arms and gave him a kiss that made Peter's toes curl.

"Come, it's time for us to go exploring."

Jarek had already lit the bedroom and Peter stopped dead in the doorway. The seduction started there. The bedroom was perfect for loving as far as Peter was concerned. He was led to the center of the room and Jarek turned to face him, giving him another kiss while roving all over his body with hands that were gentle and caressed him with infinite delicacy. The clothes started falling as their passion grew and two naked young men were clinging to each other already breathing heavily as the last articles hit the floor. The foreplay before they hit the bed had Peter gasping for Jarek's cock.

"Oh God, please fuck me. You can make love to me later, but for now just bury that fuck stick as deep as you can in my arse."

Jarek had prepared the way well. The kisses had been sensational for both of them, and when Jarek's lips followed his hands over Peter's body, the sensations from his nipples and his cockhead as Jarek licked and swallowed it, were unbelievable.

Peter knew he would want this to go on all night but before that, more than anything in the world he wanted Jarek to take his virginity. The rimming he got accompanied by fingers made him cum once, but he was still so turned on that his cock lost none of its hardness and Jarek didn't falter in his actions. Peter's entreaty brought a halt though, and Jarek lubed his cock and Peter's anus before positioning for entry. He eased over a very relaxed sphincter and was shaken rigid by the cry of joy that Peter emitted.

"Oh yes, all of you, Lover. I want all of you."

Jarek slid all the way in, amazed that there was no resistance at all. Bearing down on Peter's thighs, he was able to penetrate even deeper and nearly took Peter's sanity at the extreme pleasure of his prostate being hit on every entry, and then the pain as Jarek went into his large intestine. His next orgasm was so ferocious that Jarek was nearly tossed off him. Neither of them could tell you how many orgasms they had after that. They slept for short spells and then made love again, not falling into deep sleep until the sun was shining through the bedroom window.

It was well after noon when Jarek looked at the bedside clock. Then he tried to move and realized he was glued to Peter. He did manage to part without waking his lover, but what he saw then had him in hysterics, waking Peter. They looked into each other's eyes and then at the mess of dried cum between them. It was disgusting.

"That is all yours. I take no responsibility for any of it."

Peter moved sideways and showed Jarek the sheet.

"And that is all yours. I couldn't keep it all inside me."

The laughter died slowly and Jarek got serious. He kissed Peter with so much passion that it left Peter gasping.

"I lust you to the nth degree, Peter, but I think I love you as well. I have never made love with so much joy in my heart as last night."

Peter almost whispered, "I have never made love before, but I doubt I will ever experience anything as sensational again in my life even if I have a thousand lovers."

Despite the disgusting state of the bed and their bodies, it was another hour and several more orgasms before they headed for the shower.

"I hope you didn't have any plans for today. It is already the middle of the afternoon."

Peter grinned.

"Despite my normally heavy social commitments, I cleared my schedule for this weekend."

The eyes, full of laughter and lust accompanied that comment and Jarek buried him in more kisses.

"Well, I do have one social commitment and you are going to love joining me to it. I always have Sunday lunch with Tom and my sister-in-law. I am going to inform them there will be one extra guest this week."

Peter looked very apprehensive.

"I think I am going to love you for a long time. I am going to feed you as well and since you have committed to being my slave, you will be living here and joining me whenever I see my brother outside of work."

"Oh crikey, Jarek, what will they say?"

"I imagine Lisa will say I need to look after you because you are the most stunning young man she has ever seen and my brother will make some comment like, *'as you have picked the cutest student on campus, I presume I'm not going to be entertaining a string of my students at Sunday lunches.'* Then he will see if he can make any more embarrassing comments. Don't worry, my love, I'll rein him in if he goes too far."

For the remainder of Saturday, they just ate, made love, and went to bed exhausted but as happy as they had ever been. Curling up with Peter just for cuddles was, to Jarek, the epitome of contentment. It was two very happy young men that presented themselves at the dean's house for lunch and Jarek had been almost word perfect at Lisa's and Tom's comments.

"Seriously, Jarek, Peter isn't going to be the first of many is he?"

Peter's look of concern was back.

"No, Tom. I am as sure as I can be that when Peter graduates he will still be living with me."

"How does that sit with you, Peter?"

"I hope he means it, Dean. I have never had a boyfriend before and I am already sure that I don't want another one."

Tom looked at Lisa and then turned back to the boys.

"In that case, if he doesn't look after you, come and see me and we will jointly act as CDOs and sort him out."

Peter looked shocked.

"He means it, Peter, and you can see he is big enough to enforce it. He took over discipline in our home when mum and dad died so I have felt the force of his hand on my butt a few times when I got rebellious, and my age didn't matter. How old was I the last time you paddled my bare arse, Tom?"

Tom thought for a minute and then replied, "It was the half term before you got your bachelor's degree, so that would have made you twenty-one."

Peter was amazed.

"Are you serious, Sir? You spanked Jarek butt-naked when he was 21."

"Yes and I will do it again at 25 so you keep me in the loop if he doesn't treat you right."

They left the dean's house with Peter's head still reeling at the information he had gleaned. It also gave him a tingle at the thought of spanking Jarek.

"With such powerful support, I think I ought to become the slave master and you can be my slave. If you disobey me, I will go to Tom and let him instigate CDO punishment."

Bad move on Peter's part. Jarek said nothing but as soon as they closed the door of the apartment, he had Peter in a half nelson, stripped him naked then sat down with him over his knees. Stroking Peter's butt he spoke, "Now, what were you saying you cheeky little runt?"

"I'll tell Tom and you will be in so much trouble."

"Mmm, I think I should double my original number of slaps as you are going to be a little snitch. On the other hand, this is such a cute butt. Perhaps, I should just lick it instead of spanking it."

Peter giggled then and replied, "I wonder what punishment Tom would administer if I told him that you had put me in my place by licking my cheeks for half an hour and making me cum at least once before you stuck that big, nasty cock in between them."

"I have no idea but I'm going to do just that."

It was getting dark outside by the time Jarek had finished punishing Peter.

Peter was almost crying with happiness.

"I love you so much, Jarek. I don't think I have ever been this happy in my life."

Another passionate kiss and Jarek whispered to his little lover, "That goes double for me. I am so pleased that you were a naughty boy on my first day on the job."

Monday morning and two very happy young men went off to work together.

## Chapter 4

The weekend had not been without its moments on campus. The duty security supervisor brought two boys to the CDO's rooms at the beginning of the day and secured them both in the outer office. He dropped a report on Jarek's desk and spoke.

"The two students involved are in the outer office. You won't have any problem deciding which one is which. This wasn't a solo effort but the other students were really only there as bystanders, none of them actually took part in the attempted rape."

Jarek looked dolefully at the security supervisor.

"Alright, Fred, thank you. Leave the boys where they are and I'll deal with them after I have read this."

Without even pulling up photos of the two boys, he could almost draw a picture of them. The rapist was going to be built like a rugby player and the other boy was going to look like a stripped down racing snake, he guessed.

The reality was that Damien Carter was a post-graduate student who had been allowed to continue at college because of his incredible ability on the rugby field. Almost single-handedly, he had kept the college at the top of the rugby league. Not overly bright, he was apparently trying to organize a frat house similar to colleges in the States. The problem was that his hazing had gone too far at the weekend and he had tried to rape a junior. Chance Simmons was small enough to have his presence on campus queried frequently. He was eighteen years old but looked about fourteen. Apparently, he was an A-grade student and a bit of a loner.

After Jarek had read the report, he took it with him to the outer office and before releasing either of the students, made them read the report and comment on it.

Chance looked very embarrassed as he handed it back, and Damien, who looked older than Jarek, sneered as he handed it back and said, "Yeah, that's about it. The little cocksucker wouldn't take me in his mouth or arse so I used a bit of persuasion."

Jarek nodded, removed the recording device from his pocket and finished using it by speaking into it.

"Damian Carter has just read the security supervisor's report on his weekend action with Chance Simmons. The report indicates that Carter attempted to rape Simmons."

Carter began to look less bolshie now and squirmed at the next comment from Jarek.

"I am giving you two choices. You can accept my punishment, which I promise you will be as humiliating and sexually embarrassing as I can make it, or I can call the police and hand this report and the tape to them for further action. I think that will see you incarcerated in an adult prison for at least five years, considering the number of witnesses we have. Your choice, but know that if you balk even once at any order I give you, if you choose my punishment, I will call the police."

The mumbled reply was what Jarek expected. He was going to accept CDO punishment.

"Very well, be warned, we are going to re-enact what you tried to do to Chance, only there will be other participants. Your insides at both ends are going to be lubricated with copious quantities of man juice before we are finished."

Jarek was almost wetting himself thinking that he never expected to be able to go so far with a student. He released Chance and took him through to the inner office.

"Sit down, Chance. Give me a minute to sort my two supervisory students and then we'll talk."

Both of Jarek's first choice supervisors would be clear of lectures after lunch so he called them. Marcus and Jack heard what Jarek wanted from them and were delighted to agree. Chance heard the conversation and was wide-eyed with shock.

"Now young man, how would you like to do the same as Marcus and Jack?"

Chance thought about it for a minute and then asked a qualifying question.

"You want me to let Damien give me a blowjob to orgasm and make him swallow my sperm, and when I have recovered you want me to fuck him as well. You will guarantee my safety when I have done that?"

Jarek grinned.

"Yes, that sums it up nicely. I can guarantee Damien will never touch you again before I release him."

Chance grinned. He had been monumentally embarrassed when Damien had stripped him and played with him until he had an erection, all of it in front of the rugby squad and a few of his classmates.

"Ok, I know how to fuck so Damien's arse shouldn't pose a problem."

The two of them were giggling then like a couple of school girls. Chance thought he could easily get to like this CDO.

"Alright, Chance, you can go now, be back here at 1300. I'll keep Damien here."

Chance almost bounced on his way out, grinning at Damien as he passed him. Jarek didn't tell Damien anything. He just left him to squirm for the whole morning. He handled two minor disciplinary cases, neither of them getting beyond a few embarrassing questions while standing naked on the platform with two supervisory students present.

At 1300, Marcus and Jack walked in, closely followed by Chance. They looked at Damien and just shook their heads with doleful looks on their faces. They were briefed thoroughly in Jarek's office, the grins on their faces getting broader by the minute.

"This whole exercise is to administer maximum humiliation and embarrassment, so when you fuck him, I don't want him hurt. Use plenty of lubricant on your penises and in his arse. Are you sure you are not upset being asked to get naked and erect in front of each other?"

Marcus spoke for himself and Jack, "You know us two, Sir. We have been naked and hard in front of each other before, so there's no problem having Chance here as well."

Chance blushed a little, "I'm only a skinny little runt, Sir, but I have nothing to be ashamed of between my legs."

They all laughed at that and Jarek made Chance feel even better when he spoke, "I haven't seen you naked yet, but my guess is that you are not a runt."

"Thank you, Sir," and Chance blushed a little more, liking the CDO even more.

"Alright, Marcus, bring our criminal in."

Standing on the platform facing Jarek, Damien looked at the other three students, patently not happy.

"Let me remind you that total cooperation is required from you or you will be on your way to prison. Now, stand still while my two supervisors strip you."

Damien was about to complain when he saw the look on Jarek's face.

*'That bastard is only my age. I want to kill him,'* were his thoughts as he accepted the order.

Marcus and Jack made a real meal of stripping Damien, running their hands over his groin and arse as they removed his trousers and then, very slowly removed his briefs. Again, making sure they stroked his arse and cock as they did so. He was partially erect by the time they had finished and stood back.

Damien was blushing, and it got worse when Jarek told the two supervisors to bring him to a complete erection as he had already started to chub up.

Jack stroked Damien's arse after telling him to spread his legs wider and put his hands behind his head. He ran his fingers down the crack, worrying the anal entry. Marcus played with the balls in one hand and gently wanked the cock in the other. The result, as it would have been with any normal male, was a very hard cock that was shorter than any of the other boys present except for Jack. Jarek would make Damien squirm over that during the course of the action.

"Very nice, Carter. Chance, take a chair onto the platform and when Damien has finished undressing you and played with you to get you an erection, sit on it with your legs well spread so that he can get between your legs to give you a blowjob. Like he wanted you to do to him and his cronies."

Very reluctantly, Damien complied. By the time he had Chance erect, there were four pairs of eyes looking quite shocked. The boy was quite gorgeous. Yes, he was definitely slim, but not skinny. His body was well-defined, very pale, and his blond hair made that even more pronounced. But it was his groin that had everyone's eyes wide open. He was sporting a good seven inches of man meat and a well-hung set of balls. Jarek got hard just looking at him.

*'Christ, I wish I could touch this boy. This one is a delight to look at.'*

Then Jarek felt guilty, thinking about Peter.

He nodded at Marcus and Jack and they moved close to the action, one on each side of Chance's chair and watched as Damien started sucking him.

"He doesn't look very enthusiastic, Sir."

Marcus grinned, knowing what Jarek was going to say.

"Come up on all fours, Damien, and Marcus, five with your bare hand."

They were hard and Damien suddenly found a great deal of enthusiasm for his task. Chance was looking very happy now as Damien played with his balls, stroked his torso, and sucked on his cock. When Chance orgasmed, Jarek told Damien to swallow it all. Chance sat back after his orgasm, looking spent but happy.

"Did you enjoy that, youngster?"

"Oh yes, Sir. Damien was very good. I've never had a better orgasm."

The applause only made Damien blush, and it got worse as he blew the two supervisors as well. Interestingly, he was erect for most of it and Jarek guessed that this big, rugby-playing jock was a severe closet case.

"Stand up, Damien, and face my desk."

The whole package displayed for all to see was very impressive. The cock that was now genuinely rock-hard looked quite lethal attached to this muscled hunk.

"Gently play with yourself, Damien, and tell us why you are so rock-hard."

Damien blushed and tried to say he didn't know, but that sounded hollow even to himself.

"Is it because you have just gotten your hands on three very sexy young men with incredible groin areas that any gay man would lust after? Remember, if you lie to me and I find out, your next punishment will be infinitely worse. I will have to use the cane which will render you unfit for rugby for several weeks."

"Ok, so they are very attractive guys. In fact, I will go so far as to say Jack is beyond stunning."

"I agree, and if I weren't a master, I would be trying very hard to do what you have just done and what they are about to do to you."

The three students looked in shock at Jarek.

"Remember guys, it never leaves this room. Yes, I'm gay and I do think you are three stunning young men. Now, Damien, lie on the punishment bench on your back. Jack and Marcus, take his legs, spread them wide and pull them back then bend them so that his knees are on either side of the bench."

'*Oh Christ, I want to fuck that,*' was Jarek's thought, looking at the muscled cheeks and the anus opened for viewing.

"Chance, use the lube and open up Damien's anus until you can slide three fingers in with little resistance."

The action looked incredible. Once again, all three young students were rock-hard and Damien was almost peeing pre-cum.

"This doesn't look very much like punishment, Damien. You are patently enjoying this too much. Lube yourself, Chance, and fuck him to orgasm."

The action looked fantastic as this little chap with a not-so-little cock fucked the huge rugby player. The two of them orgasmed close together with Damien being first. He took Chance with him by working on his gluts in time with his own pulsing jets of cum.

"Straight in, Jack, he's already well-lubricated."

Jarek was amazed to see Damien hard again very quickly. Jack was too turned on to last long but Damien managed another hands-free and amazing orgasm as Marcus slow-fucked him. Damien was completely wasted and just lay where he was when Jarek sent the others off to shower and dress. When they came back, Jarek asked Chance if he felt Damien had been sufficiently humiliated and embarrassed.

"I'm not sure, Sir. Perhaps, we should do it all again," and then he sniggered before continuing, "Yes, Sir. I think that was fantastic. I've never been blown nor fucked an arse before. Both experiences were amazing, and Damien helped by having such fantastic muscle control."

"Good. In that case, Damien, your punishment is complete. Please, don't do anything silly again. I'm sure there are plenty of gay students that will be delighted to satisfy your sexual needs without having to resort to force. Thank you, Marcus and Jack. You are free now, same as you, Chance."

The boys left and Damien went for his shower and unloaded a mass of cum from his anus. When he came back, Jarek made him bend over the punishment bench.

"Spread your legs, Damien. I'm going to cream your arse so that there will be no soreness to spoil your game on the weekend."

Jarek spread Damien's cheeks to start with before releasing one and inserting one finger with an Aloe Vera cream on it. He fucked him slowly with the one finger, noting Damien getting another rock-hard erection.

"I normally wouldn't consider touching a student while he/she is in this room, but you are a post-graduate student the same age as me. If you want me to get rid of that erection for you, just roll onto the bench, spread your legs, and I will see what I can do."

Jarek went back to his desk and shut off the camcorders before returning and getting between Damien's legs. The blowjob he gave him was incredibly satisfying for both men, and Jarek knew he would have to wank himself to orgasm after Damien left.

"Christ, Jarek that is way and beyond the best blowjob I have ever had. How can I qualify for more of the same?"

"Sorry, Damien, you can't. That was definitely a one of."

Damien nodded, got dressed and put out his hand.

"Thanks. I know you could have ruined my life if you had chosen to. I'll apologize to Chance next time I see him."

# *Chapter 5*

There was not much excitement during the next few weeks. There were still the odd chancers that brighten up Jarek's life, but nothing serious. Jarek took to wandering around the campus during quiet spells, watching how the students behaved outside of lectures. He was quite surprised on several occasions to see Chance and Damien together. Curiosity killed the cat, and definitely got the better of Jarek. So one day, he intercepted them for a chat.

"I have been quite surprised to see you two together so often. Have you become friends?"

They both blushed and Jarek saw the look Damien gave Chance, it oozed with love.

"A bit more than friends, Sir, Chance and I have become lovers. I look after him and he gives me so much pleasure, just like in our punishment session."

Jarek smiled, "I can imagine. Chance has one of the most delightful penises I have ever seen."

"Yes, Sir, but so has Damien. We love to swap around when we are making love."

Chance was blushing so much Jarek thought he was going to pass out.

"I'm very pleased to hear that. I shall have to persuade my boyfriend to play swapsies occasionally. It is obviously very good for you two."

All three laughed and Jarek left them.

His last comment to the two lovers made him think. Peter did have a gorgeous cock. He loved to suck it and play with it while he was making love to him. Surely, it would feel even better roaming round the sensitive skin inside his anus. On top of which, constant stimulation of his prostate would be even better, it certainly drove Peter wild.

While he was still in a contemplative mood, Jarek bumped into the female CDO. They talked for a while swapping stories and garnering laughs from each other. When he told her the story of the two boys in the biology class and the young female professor witnessing a punishment session, it got her thinking about males witnessing a female punishment session.

"I imagine the embarrassment of just being naked in front of a female student or staff would be enough punishment."

Jarek laughed.

"You have no idea, Annette, the boys blush almost scarlet, but it gets worse when I make them get an erection and in the case of the classroom session, I even sanction some fingering. My supervisory students love it when we go far enough for them to get blowjobs. The straight boys are totally cowed after that because I tell them that next time it will be anal."

That comment got Annette seriously considering doing the same with some of the girls who didn't appear to worry about getting naked in front of her and the student supervisors. She thought about letting a boy finger them in either orifice might be enough to make sure there were no repeat performances.

"Next time I have a really hard case to deal with, Jarek, will you allow one of your supervisors to witness and take part in my punishment session?"

"Of course, I'll give you one of the heterosexual guys so that his erection will be solid."

They both laughed then and went their separate ways. Jarek tried to remember which one of his supervisors had the most impressive cock the day it all started. Danny Holmes came to mind. He was a geeky guy but he certainly qualified. Jarek had profiled all of his supervisors during the first few weeks and apparently, Danny was quite the lethal type. He was very into girls and they were into him as a bed partner.

During the period before Annette asked for a male to be present, Jarek had broached the idea to Peter of him taking the active roll.

"Making love to you, Peter, is without doubt the most wonderful thing that has ever happened to me. But I am curious what it would be like to be on the receiving end of your love stick."

"You aren't still an anal virgin are you, Lover?"

Jarek gave an embarrassed laugh, "Mmm, afraid so. I've always been the macho type in bed and never thought about it. Guys I took to bed before were just a fuck, no real attachment to them. But with you, that has all changed. I love you so much I just feel it would be good, even if it is only once, to have you inside me."

Peter had never been the active partner and being honest with himself, he was a little worried about doing it.

"I love you very much as well, but I'm not sure about doing it to you. Can I think about it?"

Jarek could see the worry on his lover's face so he moved in close and pulled him into a cuddle.

"There is no hurry, my love, and no compulsion for you to do it. Just know that if you would like to try it, I would be delighted."

Peter was a little teary-eyed and gave Jarek one of those toe-curling kisses.

Nothing more was said on the subject and Jarek kind of forgot about it.

Annette called him a week after their chat and asked if he could supply a male supervisor to attend a punishment session for a repeat offender.

"She's a very pretty girl, Jarek, and she thinks that allows her to be a pain to all her lecturers. My punishments are obviously too mild for her to desist so you and one of your studs may be able to help me."

"Sounds interesting, Danny Holmes is my choice. I'll send you his roster and you let me know when you would like us."

It was all arranged for late the following afternoon. The venue for the girls was almost a mirror image of the boys. The only major difference was that Annette had stirrups fitted to the punishment bench. She laughed at Jarek's quizzical look.

"If I use them, both of my supervisors can have a free hand to play. I try to use lesbian supervisors all the time. They really get into it, but this girl appears to be immune to the humiliation."

Danny was fascinated, thinking how much fun he could have with a girl strapped down on this contraption.

The punishment candidate looked very apprehensive when she came in escorted by a female supervisor, and saw the male CDO and a student. She was made to stand on the platform and Annette began, "My previous punishments didn't appear to work on you, Sheila, so today Mr. Howard will witness and one of his supervisors will assist."

Sheila blustered saying males couldn't be present, already knowing that they could because of the biology class session with mixed company.

"Mr. Holmes, why don't you strip our mouthy subject?"

Danny didn't need asking twice. He made a performance of it, caressing each piece of skin that he uncovered, particularly the breasts. When the girl was naked and blushing, Danny looked at Annette who just nodded, guessing what Danny wanted to do.

"Place your hands behind your head, Sheila, and move your feet further apart."

Danny grinned as she obeyed and moved his hand down to stroke the girl's pubic bush, sliding one finger along the slit of her vagina.

"I think you should feel the inside of both entry places, Danny."

Annette's comment made everyone gasp. Sheila complained bitterly while Danny showed a great deal of enthusiasm.

"That has earned you another stage of punishment, young lady. I suggest you keep your mouth shut. Continue, Danny, but use gel for the rear passage."

Danny didn't mind one bit. He had never explored the rear passage of a female but now he was. He squatted down behind the girl, made her spread her legs further, and slid a finger in. Interesting, he fingered her for a few minutes until Annette suggested he would have better access if the girl was on the punishment bench.

The female supervisor strapped Sheila down, put her legs in the stirrups and then wound them back and very wide. Danny almost came in his pants looking at the image end on.

"Five minutes, Danny, to explore."

Danny couldn't believe his luck. He was able to finger front and back at the same time with complete ease. He managed to match fingers, three front and three back before his time was up.

"Very good Danny, you can release Sheila now."

It was quite obvious that Danny was seriously aroused so Annette rendered the last punishment.

"You can undress Mr. Holmes now, Sheila."

Once naked and erect, all three females had gaping mouths. The boy was quite impressive.

A chair was placed on the platform and Danny was told to make himself comfortable.

"Now, Sheila, you can show your appreciation to Danny for being so gentle by giving him a blowjob. I want to see plenty of enthusiasm, or he may have to use it somewhere else."

Sheila looked frightened now. The thought of these other people watching while Danny used that monster to fuck her filled her with terror. The result was Danny unloading a huge amount of sperm into her mouth. He held her head to stop her from pulling off.

Job done, Danny got dressed and the two supervisors left. The girl stood in front of Jarek and Annette, looking a lot less arrogant than when she entered.

"I can think of only two more punishments worse than this one, Sheila. I am sure Danny would be delighted to return and plant his maleness in either or both of your openings."

Looking very pointedly at Sheila's lower half, Annette left no doubt which openings she meant.

"You may use the bathroom, get dressed, and pray that you are never sent to me again."

After she had gone, Annette asked Jarek what he thought.

"I know from the experience in the biology lecture that my workload decreased significantly after it. Some chancers will risk the humiliation in front of their own sex, but they are not so keen at the thought of the opposite being present. I shall have to invite you to witness one of my more extreme punishment sessions if another one occurs."

Jarek walked back to his office thinking about the stirrups. He was sure that a boy secured in one of those setups would be monumentally embarrassed, opened up for viewing in that way. It would also be the perfect position if he ever went the whole hog and had a supervisor fuck a delinquent student. So stirrups were ordered and installed a few weeks later. Jarek was eager to try them but realized they had to be for a serious breach of discipline.

The end of term was very close when a student decided to strike his classmate in the middle of a lecture. The student that was struck was Asian and didn't retaliate. This, for Jarek was the perfect situation. He sent for the Asian student first.

Tang was studying psychology and had chosen this college because outside of Japan, it offered the finest training. He was a serious martial arts student as well. Under Jarek's interrogation, he found out that Tang had not retaliated because, according to him, *'In the limited space that the incident afforded, I would have been hard pressed to be certain that I would not seriously damage my aggressor, so I did not strike back,'*

Jarek looked at the clothed student and thought he was probably correct.

"I have every intention of rendering my most severe punishment for this offence. It will be easy for me to allow one of my supervisors to carry it out, but I feel it'll be more impressive if I'm able to persuade you to do it. The punishment will entail Alan Maidment giving a blowjob and then being butt-fucked. If you want to be the recipient, I will sanction it. The witnesses will be myself, the female CDO, and two student supervisors.

Tang grinned.

"In some secret societies in my country, justice is sought by wrestling for the fuck so I am quite happy to take part where I know it isn't me that will be penetrated."

Tang had a broad grin on his face as he said that. He was soon joined by Jarek, who now had the chance to put on a real display for Annette.

Arrangements completed, Jarek asked Marcus and Jack to be his student witnesses. He knew he was doing them a favour because they were gay and instant erection material when he had them naked, not that he envisaged that happening this time.

When Alan Maidment walked in, Jarek recognised him. He was one of the rugby stars in the college team. He looked very apprehensive when he saw the audience. He had expected the two student witnesses but not Tang and the female CDO. As he stood on the platform, he looked around uneasily until Jarek spoke when he focused on what was being said. He knew he was in for a hard time, but even he had not come up with what Jarek intended.

"Listen very carefully, Maidment, because there is no leeway for you. Violence towards another student or lecturer whilst in lectures will garner my most severe punishment. If you balk at anything today, I will simply double the worst part of the punishment. I want you to follow the orders of my two supervisors while they prepare you. I will be asking questions that will be answered truthfully, because if you lie to me and I find out, I will bring you back here and have all my student supervisors to take advantage of your body."

Alan gulped. This was far worse than he had anticipated after he had let his quick temper take control.

Marcus and Jack moved on to the platform and started to strip Alan. They told him how to stand and move as required to make their job easy. Removing trousers and underpants required a huge amount of touching of his vital parts, making sure he had an erection before they finished. He had nothing to be ashamed of as he displayed a very nice set of tackle.

"How long is your penis when erect as it is now?"

Alan gulped. Of course he had measured it, what guys didn't.

"6 ½ inches, Sir."

"Very nice, and how often do you masturbate to orgasm?"

Blushing very red and looking at Annette, he replied, "A couple of times a day, Sir."

"Do you think of boys when you masturbate?"

A very rapid and shocked, "No, Sir," followed making Jarek smile.

"Have you ever used fingers or a dildo in your anus during sex?"

Again, a very rapid, "No, Sir," followed.

"Tang, to the platform, please. Alan, undress Tang. Make sure that you play with him enough to get him an erection and let him get comfortable. Then I want you to give him an amazingly enthusiastic blowjob, paying lots of attention to his balls as well. I'm sure you know how to turn on a man sexually."

Jarek smiled at that because it could be interpreted in two ways.

The result was better than Jarek expected. First, Tang had an absolutely stupendous body. Easily the best Jarek had ever seen, and it didn't stop there. His penis was far bigger than he had expected on an

Asian student. It had to be eight inches with a very attractive ball sac hanging below, and that would make the exhibition even better. Looking at Jack and Marcus he realized that they were as turned on as he was.

Alan could not remember ever being this embarrassed and he had an awful gut feeling that it was going to get worse. Common assault was what he was guilty of and that carried a prison term. Refusal to obey the CDO would also carry a term of imprisonment so he was in a no win situation, he would have to obey however bad it got. He got on his knees in between Tang's legs and started. He knew what turned him on and just re-enacted the action. He proved he was a straight boy by going completely flaccid. Blowing another guy was definitely a turn off for him. Tang's expression went from smug, to surprise, then to pleasure, to the point where he gently stroked Alan's hair. The orgasm when it came was a sight for sore eyes to the audience. Tang nearly choked Alan as he thrust deep into his throat a few times towards the end before unloading a huge orgasm deep in his mouth. There was no chance of pulling off and as he gulped it down, tears came to Alan's eyes. Eating another man's cum was the most awful thing he could think of and it was about to get even worse.

"I'm sure you would like a little time to recover, Tang, so I will let my supervisors prepare Maidment for the next action. Marcus, Jack, punishment bench, stirrups and straps."

Everyone was intrigued, even Alan as he was laid out on the punishment bench with his calves strapped into the stirrups. They were wound back and wide before he was moved down the bench so that his arse hung over the edge. Straps were then placed over his chest and hips so that he could not move and his wrists were fastened onto the side of the bench, level with his head. Alan realised that his anus, cock, and balls were on clear display to the audience who had all stood up and moved round to get perfect viewing. He watched Annette as she viewed him from every angle, with a smile on her face.

"Marcus and Jack will open up the anus of your plaything, Tang, and when you are ready again, lube your penis and fuck Alan to an orgasm."

Marcus and Jack hoped above hope that Alan would complain so that Jarek could offer them a go at his arse with their cocks that were straining to get out.

Tang was obviously sexually aroused by boy-boy sex because he was erect again very quickly and wandered round, watching Alan from every angle the same as Annette. He was fascinated watching Marcus and Jack at work, fingering the captive and playing with him as well.

Alan closed his eyes but as the long, slender fingers of Marcus found his prostate and played with it, he started elongating and ended up with the hardest erection he could remember.

*'Oh my God, that is amazing. Now I know why gay guys like to be fucked.'*

That thought made Alan question his sexuality for the first time ever. It got worse as the two students alternated in fingering him, adding one more finger each time until they had four fingers going in and out and rotating. Jarek could see Alan secreting pre-cum so he told Tang to take over and use his man rammer.

*'This boy is good,'* was Jarek's thought as he watched Tang enter Alan slowly and then long-stroked him, rotating his hips as he entered.

"Oh God, fuck me hard," was almost screamed by Alan as he had a mighty orgasm.

Everyone was surprised and applauded the request, watching in amazement as Tang sped up and power-fucked Alan until he had a mighty orgasm that made him black out, falling over Alan's torso into the mess of cum. He came to quite quickly and looked around at all the surprised faces, blushing heavily.

"I'm so sorry. I got a little carried away."

That caused almost hysterical laughter until Jarek managed to splutter out, "Really, I would never have guessed."

Alan looked around and in a very embarrassed voice stated, "I'm not gay, I'm not."

Jarek realized from the tone that he had an emotional crisis to deal with, so he sent Tang and the two witnesses to the bathroom to clean up. Marcus and Jack were so turned on that they both exploded in their trousers. He ushered them all out of the office as quickly as he could, including Annette, before approaching the platform again. He used a warm cloth to clean up the mess over Alan's torso and around his arse before winding the stirrups down and releasing the straps. He stroked the boy's torso very gently and spoke to him.

"The power of the prostate is frequently underestimated, Alan. Your genitals will almost always react to it once stimulated. None of your reproductive organs know the difference between male and female stimulation so being brought to orgasm by stimulation of your prostate is as normal as it gets. Don't freak out about your sexuality. If you start fancying guys then there is a good chance you are gay. If you just like the idea of incredible orgasms by yourself, you can always use your own fingers or buy a vibrator. There is nothing wrong with any of that. Are you ok with it?"

Alan nodded, but didn't look convinced. Jarek touched his cheek and stroked it gently. Alan looked lost.

"Please, don't get uptight about this. Come and talk to me if you have a problem. I'm more than just a punisher. Your welfare is important to me as well."

Alan nodded and then asked, "May I go and shower now?"

Jarek nodded and let him go. After he left, Jarek decided to talk to Alan's dorm mate and then possibly other members of the rugby squad. He didn't want to risk this experience toppling the boy's equilibrium. By the end of term, Jarek was reasonably happy with Alan's state of mind so no worries.

# Chapter 6

Jarek now had two weeks to concentrate on loving Peter. The only odd thing was the planned visit to Tom during Christmas but that was all. They engaged in unbridled sex all day if they had the staying power, and Jarek hoped part of that would be him losing his anal virginity.

Peter had decided that as part of his Christmas present to Jarek he would take his anal virginity. He prepared for it by really concentrating on what Jarek did to him, particularly once Jarek's cock entered him. He loved the long, slow fuck with Jarek rotating his hips to enter from a slightly different angle every time. He also loved it when Jarek had him on all fours, with his head and shoulders dropped onto his arms, to be rimmed. He could tongue-fuck Jarek as he used fingers to open him up. Then he would take him in the missionary position so that he could watch his eyes, play with his cock and balls, and lean forward occasionally for a kiss.

It happened on Christmas Eve. By the time he let Jarek orgasm, Peter had done so twice. He had never been so turned on. It was amazing watching Jarek's reaction to all the stimulation. He knew that much of that would be because it was a first, as it had been with him when Jarek took his virginity. Nonetheless, it was an amazing experience and as they cuddled afterwards with Peter still embedded in his love, Jarek told him how he felt.

"Would you like to do that every time we make love? That was quite the most incredible experience I have ever had."

Peter was so happy that he had satisfied his lover. He just buried Jarek in kisses.

"Mmm, a tempting thought, but I couldn't give up what we have had for the last three months. Your cock is to die for, but I might reciprocate occasionally if you are a good boy."

Love could at times be overwhelming, and this was one of those times for both of these young men. It became another night of lovemaking in between short spells of sleep. Jarek was unused to being penetrated so by the time they crawled out of bed to shower, he was quite sore. He wasn't sure how many times they had made love, swapping top and bottom each time. Peter made it all better for him by using an Aloe Vera cream on his insides, bringing him another orgasm.

Tom had no problem guessing how the two boys had spent the night. They were positively glowing when they turned up for Christmas lunch, bringing presents with them. Tom and Lisa had never had children, so lunch was the four of them plus two overseas students who had nowhere else to go for the holidays. One of those was Tang, who was quite surprised to realize that the CDO had a student lover. The other was an overseas student from Brazil. The boy was slim and rather plain to look at, but Jarek and Peter's eyes were drawn to his trousers. They were obviously tailored because they fitted perfectly, showing a very cute butt and an almost obscene bulge at the front. Even Lisa couldn't avoid looking at it once or twice. The young man, Paulo, was a second year student and during the course of the day, Jarek and Peter came to the distinct impression that he was either gay or asexual because he ignored any talk of girls or passed it off with disdain. It also became obvious that Tang was at least gay friendly.

Back at Jarek's apartment, he and Peter sat and talked about their impressions of the day.

"I hope Paulo will be a naughty boy sometime next term. I would love to see that bulge erect and bare."

Peter grinned and replied, making sure he let Jarek know how he really felt, "I love you more than I ever thought possible, and I have never wanted to explore other guys. Our sex life is totally amazing, but I'm also like you. I would love to have him here to play with. I wouldn't want to do anything with him without you here as well, but it could be interesting."

Jarek thought about it.

"I know that next term I will need to replace some of my seniors with second year students so that I don't interrupt their revision for finals. I can get him to do the same as I did with the original bunch, so I will get our wish. I will just have to try to find out if he is gay. If he is, I can invite him here for dinner and playtime. Sound ok with you?"

Peter grinned.

"Mmm, sounds good. Wouldn't you like to do the same with Tang? After what you told me, I would like to see him naked and erect as well."

Jarek laughed.

"We had better be careful or we could turn into cock sluts."

Both of them were laughing as Peter went, "Ooh yes, please."

The remainder of the holidays was more of the same for Jarek and Peter, lots of loving, very little socializing, except with Tom and Lisa. Peter's parents lived abroad so he only saw them once or twice a year, usually in the summer.

First day of the new term and Jarek had a directive to act on that would keep him very busy all term. He was being asked to put on paper his plan for CDO training as his first term results had been so spectacular. What he did was compile a lecture program using cuts from his DVD collection, plus notes of his mind set for different situations. Annette was brought in to add her perspective to it all from the female side.

"Apparently, Annette, the plan is for you and me to undertake a training program at the end of this term. When I am away, you will carry out the male CDO duties and vice versa."

Jarek laughed.

"I'm sure you will have more fun than me because I'm gay and you aren't."

That made Annette grin with a surfeit of pleasure at the thought. She could handle young men with erect cocks, but not literally.

With just two minor disciplinary events that first week, Jarek had loads of time improving his program notes. During the second week, Annette called him.

"You won't believe this, Jarek. Sheila let her temper get the better of her today and struck a lecturer. The professor concerned has a black eye. I have talked to a local judge who told me that if she comes before him on the assault charge, he will make an example of her and send her down for three years. I have informed the girl, and now we have to devise a punishment that will take her to the edge of accepting it. Let me have your thoughts, Jarek, will you?"

Jarek immediately thought about young Danny. He sent for him at the end of his lecture.

"Danny, come in. Sit down and make yourself comfortable. I need your help with a problem. The girl you received a blowjob from has offended again by striking a professor. The female CDO and I need the most humiliating punishment possible as an alternative to sending her to prison for three years."

Danny thought about what he had done before, jumped further with it and came up with this.

"Well, Sir, I got a blowjob, which was a good start and then I was allowed to finger her pussy and her anus. To take that further, a cock replacing the fingers would be an advance and a further advance would be a cock in each orifice so you would need three willing males. I doubt that would be difficult to find."

Jarek wondered how they could get a cock in the vagina and at the same time one in the arse. Danny told him, and then demonstrated the bit that Jarek couldn't see from his description. He lay on the punishment bench, pulled his legs back and wide.

"Now, if you straddle me, Sir, with your knees on either side of my arse, if you lean forward you could put your cock in my vagina, if I had one," and they both laughed. "Then the second male could stand behind me and fuck my arse. The third guy would be able to get a blowjob standing beside the bench."

Jarek hopped down and helped Danny stand up again.

"That is very ingenious. I will suggest it to the other CDO and if we go ahead on that basis, I will use you even though you are no longer one of my supervisors as a reward for your input."

Danny was very hard just thinking about it.

"Thank you, Sir. I promise to be very enthusiastic. Sheila is, after all, a very attractive lady."

Jarek thought the same from a purely aesthetic point of view.

"Ok, run along and I'll get back to you as soon as we finalize the punishment."

Annette was tickled by the scenario that Jarek proposed to her.

"Very ingenious, how did you think of that as a gay man?"

Jarek laughed and told her about Danny.

"I guess if I'd ever have one of the boys misbehaving so badly, I could always use the same positioning to have him double-fucked."

Annette's eyes came out on organ stops for that comment.

"Oh please, let me be present if that ever happens. That would be amazing, I'm sure."

Two people were definitely in tune here; one gay, one straight, and one of each sex. They made a good team and were beginning to realize how that made them more effective. Something else for Jarek to put into his planning notes.

Jarek sat and thought about the three males he would need, Danny for sure and two of his supervisors. Desmond would be interesting. He was a final year student and wrestler, well-endowed as one would expect from his race, very definitely straight so he would love this. Now, who for a third? He ran through his list wanting a straight man with a good size appendage.

Alec came to mind. He was a mean little sod. Jarek was sure he had a sadistic streak so he could be ideal. The boy had almost white hair that stood to attention however long it got. The asset that Jarek wanted was his cock. Not enormously long, but very thick with a very prominent glans.

The thinking now was that Danny could use his tool to fuck Sheila's arse while Alec fucked her vagina and Desmond choked her to death with his black monster. What he didn't envisage was Annette taking charge of the action and rotating them. She told him afterwards that she was so incensed at the girl striking a professor that she wanted maximum humiliation and finally pain.

The time was agreed. Jarek interviewed the two supervisors to make certain they were up for it. Jarek walked his three boys through to Annette's suite and was surprised to see two of the girl supervisors there as well. She whispered to Jarek, "These two are lesbians and this is a reward for them."

Annette started.

"Listen very carefully, Sheila. A judge has confirmed that you are facing 3 years in an adult prison if we take this assault to court. The alternative is that you accept every act carried out on you today without complaint."

Sheila said nothing so Annette continued.

"Confirm that you are on the pill and have taken it without a break for at least a month, including last night's one."

The girl was almost wetting herself with terror now.

"Desmond and Alec, please strip the girl naked. Check that she has nothing secreted into any orifice."

Desmond had three fingers in her vagina within seconds after the last piece of clothing had been removed. Alec had gone behind, made her spread her legs so wide that she almost fell over and then quite aggressively, finger-fucked her arse for a couple of minutes before returning to the front and making her suck the fingers that had been in her arse, revolting, Jarek thought.

"Now Sheila, I want you to undress the three young men in turn and show us how much improved your blowjobs are. You can start on Danny, who you pleasured last time."

Danny loved it. Desmond was next and he had her deep-throating his ten inches by the time he shot deep in her throat. Alec was last, confirming Jarek's thought. He power-fucked her mouth continually, making her gag. The four audience applauded, making the boys blush with pleasure and Sheila with embarrassment. She had swallowed each boy's cum having been given no choice. Each of them had made her keep sucking gently after they had cum until they were quite soft.

"Thank you, boys. I'm sure Sheila now has the experience to satisfy her future boyfriends. Now girls, while the boys are recovering, you can get Sheila ready for the next part of her punishment."

Jarek could see that they had been well briefed because they had Sheila on the punishment bench very quickly with her legs spread very wide in the stirrups, her body pulled forward so that her rear protruded over one end. The boys would have unfettered access to her two orifices. Her legs were wound well back so that her knees almost touched the bench on either side of her head. A waist strap was put in place so that she could not slide up the table. The girls stood at the bottom end to examine their work before moving to the side to give the audience a clear view of the vagina and anus as they stroked her breasts before moving down to finger her vagina and her arse. The sight very quickly had the three boys erect again.

"Danny, why don't you lube your penis and see if you can bury it in Sheila's arse."

Danny looked so eager Jarek had to stifle a laugh. Moving round to the side, they all watched as Danny did what he was told. It looked incredible, and Sheila let them know that this was not the hole normally used. She squealed initially but then settled down to take the whole of Danny's baby maker. Annette let it go on for a few minutes before suggesting to Desmond that he might like to try another blowjob. Again, there was no problem and the final act that had the two lesbian students almost wetting themselves was when Alec was invited to get onto the bench, straddling Sheila's legs and enter her vagina. It patently wasn't the most comfortable position, but Alec used it to good effect with his fat penis to power into Sheila and make her squeal again. After about five minutes when Alec and Danny were about ready to orgasm, Annette spoke, "Alright boys, time to change round. Danny to her mouth, Alec to her arse, Desmond to her vagina."

Jarek thought, *'Oh my god, that fat monster in her arse and Desmond's 10 inches in her vagina is going to drive her crazy.'* And he wasn't wrong. The stimulation from the two huge cocks inside her made her orgasm several times before Annette changed them round for the third time, telling them they were to orgasm this time.

Despite the fact that he was gay, Jarek was nursing a very hard penis watching the action and when Desmond slid his monster from her arse to finish it, he came in his trousers. Thankfully, he had wrapped his cock in tissue to absorb it.

The boys used the bathroom to clean up before dressing. When they were dismissed, they thanked Annette and Jarek most profusely.

"Remember the rule boys. If one word of this leaks out, you experience much worse than this from a bunch of gay guys."

They all laughed and assured Jarek that wasn't going to happen.

Jarek thought that was it and was preparing to leave as well when Annette spoke, "Ok girls, twenty."

He stood, mouth agape as he watched the two lesbian students deliver ten hard slaps each to Shiela's arse, making her scream with pain. Punishment complete and Sheila was released before the girls left.

"When you are ready you can shower, dress, and go. If I see you in this room again, you will be more than a little sorry."

Annette turned to Jarek then and grinning, said, "I hope you enjoyed the entertainment and will reciprocate at an appropriate time."

'Wow, what a session that was,' was Jarek's thought as he walked back to his own rooms. The action, however evil you considered it, had saved a young woman from a three-year jail term.

Peter was gaping when, that night, Jarek gave him a complete run down on the action.

"Oh my God, those cocks sound marvelous. Can you put me through the same thing with them?"

Then he collapsed over Jarek laughing like an idiot.

"Of course, I can," said Jarek, "If you strike one of your professors."

Peter looked at him a little cockeyed and replied, "Mmm, it might be worth it with old Doggett."

Jarek knew the professor he meant. The man was a miserable individual and a boring and pedantic lecturer. He als knew he could never put Peter through that as a punishment.

"If you really want it, I can invite them here and see if they will do the same for a boy."

Peter got serious then. "No, I think I can forgo that pleasure."

He laughed and enjoyed loving sex with Jarek when they went to bed.

# Chapter 7

'Be careful what you wish for,' was the saying that came home to roost for Peter quite early the next term. He got into a fight with another student during a lecture. The lecturer deliberately tried to raise the temperature of the debate and managed to make it go further than anticipated.

Both young men concerned were sent immediately to the CDO and the lecturer appraised Jarek of the incident.

"They should be in your outer office by the time I have finished, Jarek. They are equally to blame and neither of them admits to throwing the first punch. I personally think that the one who started it should receive the most severe punishment."

Jarek thanked him and then checked the rosters. He thought that if he could get two supervisors straightaway, he could carry out the punishment without delay. Perfect, Marcus and Jack were on late lectures that day so he called them. Both were immediately available so he told them to secure the two bad boys on the chairs as they came through the outer office.

"I don't very often let you two boys loose on the bad boys, but as we have two in for fighting, I have decided that you can both get blowjobs today and wield the cp for a dose of pain as well, as the humiliation they will take. If they balk at the action at all, you might even get some anal work for your penises, you will certainly get some for your fingers."

Marcus and Jack were erect already just thinking about it. Marcus was not slow announcing his pleasure, "Oh gosh, thank you so much, Sir. Both guys are really cute freshmen."

Jarek laughed and told them to go and collect the miscreants.

Standing on the platform facing Jarek, he looked up and gasped. Peter was looking straight back at him looking very embarrassed. Jarek knew, based on his records, that Peter was a repeat offender which meant extra punishment.

Could he avoid any anal play? Realistic answer, no. If he showed any favouritism the two seniors would know because they had access to the records as well. Jarek had always kept them all informed so that the degree of fairness, and his consistent standards would be known. Neither Jack nor Marcus knew of the relationship between the two.

Looking at the boy, he didn't know he asked his name.

"Tim Campbell, Sir."

"Marcus and Jack, take both young men back to the other room while I check their records."

Jarek looked up Tim and found he was a model student. He already knew Peter's record. He summoned Peter again, making the others remain in the outer office.

"I love you so much, but I have to be seen to be totally dispassionate and fair in dealing with you because when it eventually becomes known that we are lovers, I must not have appeared to be lenient with you."

"I know, Babe, I'm sorry. I promise that whatever punishment you hand out, I won't let it make any difference to us afterwards."

"You don't understand, Peter. Because it is a second offence and a serious one, even if you didn't throw the first punch, I will have to allow anal intercourse."

Peter looked a little shocked before nodding his head.

"I didn't, but I did throw a few before we were parted."

"In that case, I can make it less embarrassing by making Tim take cock as well."

Peter nodded and tears came to his eyes as he realized how he had let Jarek down.

Tim was brought in and Jarek told Marcus and Jack to undress the other two. Tim knew that Peter had been here before so he followed his lead, not saying anything as the two seniors stripped him. Standing naked with their legs astride and their hands grasped behind their heads, Jarek started the questioning.

"I am sure you are aware of the rules so don't even consider the idea of lying to me, or objecting to further actions. I take no pleasure in what I am going to order today because for fighting, it is going to be as bad as I can make it. You can expect pain and humiliation before you leave here."

Tim looked worried.

"Campbell, how often do you masturbate?"

Tim looked flustered, remembered the brief and softly replied, "About twice a day, Sir, if my girlfriend isn't putting out."

"Same question, Chambers."

"Never, Sir, because I have a regular partner."

Jarek blushed then.

"We intend to find out, Campbell. But before we do, how long is your erect penis and has it ever been blown?"

Tim blushed like crazy.

"Seven inches, Sir, and yes."

Jarek was going to ask what sex the cocksucker was but didn't want Peter to have to say male if Tim said female.

"Same question, Chambers."

"Seven and a half, and yes."

"Marcus and Jack, take one each and get them erections. Here is a tape measure, confirm their estimates."

Jarek could see that Peter didn't mind this part at all. Tim, however, was embarrassed and took longer to reach a full erection. Peter was incredibly hard. He loved Marcus' soft hands playing with his cock and balls.

"Chambers lied a little, Sir, he is closer to 8 than 7 ½."

"Campbell is just about spot on, Sir."

Jarek could see that both his boys were delighted with this first part of the punishment.

"Very good, chairs on the platform, Campbell and Chambers, undress the seniors and then, when they are comfortable, I want to see you blow them to orgasm."

Tim looked gutted but once again followed Peter's lead.

Jarek was going to take Peter to task that night. He was enjoying blowing Marcus much more than he should. Then again, if he could, Jarek would blow Marcus as well.

Task completed with Marcus and Jack grinning like idiots.

"I presume they were satisfactory."

Marcus just kept grinning, Jack tried to look serious.

"I think Campbell could do with some more practice, Sir. I would be willing to take him for lessons."

Jarek found it really difficult not to laugh as he replied, "I will take that offer under advisement. The next part of the punishment will depend on your answer to my next question, Campbell, who threw the first punch?"

Tim looked at Peter first before replying, "I did, Sir. I'm really sorry. Peter just got me so wound up that I lashed out without thinking."

"Do you agree with that comment, Chambers?"

Peter actually liked Tim. They normally got on well together and Peter thought he was cute, but straight.

"Yes, Sir, I guess I did better than Professor Blair expected, since he wanted some fire in the debate."

"To put it crudely, you both need some sense to be fucked into you, Campbell for landing the first blow, and you Chambers as a repeat offender. Because violence is involved, you will both be paddled as well. Marcus and Jack, Campbell first on the bench. Open him up and when you think he is ready, one of you can penetrate him."

There were four very hard cocks as Tim was opened up, being played with at the same time until his cock was as hard as the others.

Peter and Jarek kept swapping glances. Peter could see the anguish on Jarek's face and felt like shit.

When Jack entered Tim, Jarek thought, '*Damn, I should have specified Marcus. He is longer than me so he will be felt more by Peter.*'

The reality was that Peter would love having Marcus' long cock reaming him out.

Watching Jack fuck Tim to orgasm made Jarek orgasm as well, though he had been prepared and the sticky mess was confined to the tissues he was encased in. Tim looked totally embarrassed because he had remained erect throughout. Jack had been constantly caressing his prostate on every entry.

"Your turn, Marcus."

Jarek couldn't look Peter in the eyes. He did, however, watch very intently as Marcus enjoyed an incredible fuck. Peter worked his gluts to enhance the sensuality for Marcus who looked at him quizzically. Peter had a wonderful orgasm almost at the same time as Marcus, who fell forward onto Peter after cumming. Peter whispered in his ear, "Thanks, Marcus. That was pretty damn good," and then he grinned.

Marcus and Jack went to shower and dress while Peter and Tim stood back on the platform waiting for the next bit.

"I seldom use the paddle because I take no pleasure in rendering pain. But fighting demands that from my own code. I am, however, going to limit it to five each and my seniors will administer it."

When Marcus and Jack came back, Jarek gave them each a paddle and told them they could choose the position to administer the punishment. He whispered to them that they were not to use too much force.

"Five each, please, to complete the punishment."

Jack simply made Tim bend over and touch his toes before landing five, medium strength strokes on his butt. They patently hurt but not enough for Tim to move. Marcus had Peter bend over the punishment bench and Jarek could see that there was little strength in the strokes, barely marking Peter's arse.

Peter and Tim were then sent for showers and Jarek spoke to his seniors.

"I presume, Marcus, the paddling was a thank you to Peter for a great fuck."

Marcus grinned.

"The best I have ever had, Sir. I think I can guarantee that Peter Chambers is one of us."

Jarek nearly fell over laughing but managed to splutter out, "I agree. What about Campbell?

"A nice heterosexual boy is my guess, Sir. He didn't enjoy any of it."

Tim and Peter came back and were allowed to dress before Jarek addressed them again.

"Both of you have been subjected to the most severe punishment I have had to render up to now. A third offence for you, Peter, is not something you should even think about because it will be even worse than today. And for you Tim, since your first offence is so severe, you can think in terms of something worse as well. The 'what,' I will leave to your imaginations."

Everyone filed out and Marcus walked alongside Peter.

"I think you are an incredible sex machine, Peter. I would love to get together with you in private to find out how much better you could be."

"I'm flattered, Marcus, and if I didn't love my partner so much I would jump at the invitation. The best I can offer is that I will talk to him and see if he would go for a threesome. Don't hold your breath though because he is in a position that I am sure will make him say, no."

"Pity you are seriously cute as well."

Peter grinned. "Mmm, that's what he says too."

Jarek was taken aback when Peter told him of that conversation that night.

"His cock did feel incredible roving around inside me, Babe. I wouldn't mind feeling it again, but only with you present. I'm not looking for sex with anyone else unless you are there."

Jarek felt the same as Peter but he thought having sex with Marcus would complicate his life too much.

"Perhaps, at the end of the year once I replace Marcus to do his finals."

Peter hugged himself after that comment. Something to look forward to and he could tell Marcus felt that as well.

Just after half-term, Jarek was summoned by the powers that be to show them what he had achieved with regards to the training program.

"Mr. Howard, your success at the college has been astounding. Educational stats have improved to an incredible level, and your punishment log is beginning to look very sparse. We would like you to do your first training course at the end of term with the idea that we should put fifty more CDOs in place for the final term of the year."

Jarek was delighted. The final comment was even better.

"Once you start your first training course your new title will be, *Director of Discipline Training*, with a salary commensurate with the new responsibility. Looking further forward, we may leave you in your present location but appoint a junior CDO to run things when you are away, and also for that person to be groomed by you as a permanent deputy. You will be able to select the candidates. We will advertise the position and whittle the applicants down to 100. You can eliminate 50 and train the rest. We'll call you to do that as soon as we have the numbers."

Jarek went back home almost walking on air. He had a job that fitted his psyche perfectly. Well, not entirely perfect. He would love to get his hands on some of the young men sent to him for punishment. He wondered if that would ever be allowed. At college level, all students were legal for sex, homo or straight so he could actually see no reason why he shouldn't get involved as long as he always had at least one other student as a witness. Perhaps he would recommend it, with the excuse that the CDOs would have so much more experience and bring another level to the punishments for the seriously hard cases. Like Peter, he sniggered this.

He told Tom when he arrived home. He didn't tell him about the angle he was working on though, because he knew Tom would disapprove knowing that he was gay. He was completely wrong. Tom obviously reviewed the logs and congratulated Jarek on being totally professional in the way he dealt with Peter.

"There may be times as you deal with the really hard-core disrupters when it would be a good move for the CDOs to get hands-on. They will be much more experienced than the student supervisors and be able to bring a higher level of humiliation and embarrassment to the proceedings. If they are gay like you, Jarek, I imagine you can make certain that the hardest nut didn't want to come back for say a fourth of fifth punishment. It is bad enough up to three or two if violence is involved. I can only imagine what else you're capable of, and I'm a straight man."

Jarek didn't know what to say initially and then got his act together.

"Tom, will you send that suggestion to me as a memo? I will have a report from Annette concerning the female side quite soon and I will forward your memo with her notes and see what the committee says."

Jarek had his fingers crossed then that his thoughts and Tom's suggestion would become reality.

---

When Jarek told Peter, the laughter at Peter's comments could be heard all the way to campus, well, nearly.

"Ooh, let me know when it happens then I can have sex with you at college just by being a naughty boy, and it will all be condoned and legal."

The sex they had that night was as good as always. It was amazing that just by talking about it could have them both so horny.

Jarek had so much time now to refine his training program. He also started to give some thought to more advanced punishments for the small number of hard-core disrupters that would hang on in college rather than go out to work. Walks around the campus continued and he was pleased to bump into Paulo one day. He hadn't seen him since the day at Tom's.

"Hello, Paulo. How are you?"

Paulo smiled at seeing Jarek again.

"I'm very well, Sir, and it's so good to see you again."

Jarek laughed.

"Well, you can see me any time, just be a naughty boy and I'll see you in the CDO's rooms."

Paulo laughed as well and then looked at Jarek through hooded eyes as he replied, "Well, I've heard some exciting things happening there so perhaps, I will."

Jarek was interested in that comment. No one was supposed to talk about punishment sessions. The only public one had been the two boys in the biology class.

"What time are you free of lectures today?"

Paulo replied that he was already free. He only had one lecture this day.

"Ok, I would like you to come back with me. I have some questions I'd like answered."

Paulo was intrigued and walked back with Jarek to his CDO suite.

Sitting comfortably, Jarek started, "You know that what happens here is not meant to leave here. I can't imagine any of the bad boys talking about their experiences so I presume that whatever you have heard has come from one of my supervisory students. What I would like to know is what you have heard."

The story Paulo told covered stripping, masturbating, and blowjobs. But none of the penetrations or the ones witnessed by Annette or by the boys in Annette's punishment sessions were mentioned.

"Alright, now I need to know who told you."

"I wasn't told by anyone, Sir, just what I overheard."

"I would still like to know who it was."

"I'm sorry. I don't think I can do that."

"You know that I have a *carte blanche* on punishment. I could make you strip, masturbate, give one of my seniors a blowjob, even let one of them have anal intercourse with you."

Paulo looked stunned.

"I didn't realize you could go that far but I'm sorry. I still can't tell you."

Jarek smiled.

"Much as I would like to see you naked, erect and giving a blowjob to some lucky student, I don't intend to."

Paulo relaxed then and smiled.

"Spoilsport, I know some of your supervisors. They are a pretty sexy bunch."

Jarek could see the funny side of that comment and also the fact that Paulo called his boys sexy.

"Why don't you come to dinner at my place on Friday night? You can stay over if you want to. I have a spare bedroom."

"I would like that very much."

"Good, I'll come and pick you up at 7 outside your dorm, if that is ok. And I'll be Jarek for the weekend."

# Chapter 8

That was how it was left and Jarek told it to Peter.

"If we are crafty, we might be able to see what he is packing."

Sex hounds showed their true colours!

Of course, Paulo knew that Jarek and Peter were friends. What he hadn't realized was that they were living together in a gay relationship. It didn't take him long to notice though, when he saw the domestic setup and heard them talking to each other. He blushed with the realization, picked up by Jarek.

"Although it's not illegal for Peter to be my partner, Paulo, we don't make it known at college. The dean knows of course, but I would appreciate it if you don't let it become general knowledge."

Paulo laughed.

"Of course not, for you that must make the CDO job the best in the world then."

Jarek laughed with him and replied, "Actually, it's the most frustrating job in the world. I can look but not touch, and being a voyeur doesn't cut it for me."

Paulo hadn't realized that Jarek could order all the sexual punishments but not indulge himself.

"Crikey, in that case, I don't think I'll volunteer for the CDO program when I graduate. I would go crazy letting my imagination turn things into reality but not be able to indulge."

The words were hardly out of his mouth before he realized he had effectively told Jarek and Peter that he was gay as well.

Peter jumped in then, "I'm sure Jarek wouldn't mind if we role-played a few sessions here if you would like to have some fun."

Paulo didn't know what to say but managed to stutter out, "How would that work with just the three of us?"

Jarek laughed.

"I would change the rules so that the CDO could indulge as well and only use one senior witness instead of the usual two or I could bring in one of my seniors and do it right."

Looking very shy, Paulo said, "Could we?"

"Of course, we are free tomorrow so if you would like to stay tonight, we could play after breakfast in the morning. We could even have a simple session this evening after dinner if you would like."

A very enthusiastic, "Oh yes, please," solved that one.

Tom had continued teaching Jarek how to cook after their parents died. He continued to learn and improve while he was in college, so dinner was a very pleasant meal, washed down with a decent wine. All cleared away afterwards and Jarek set the criteria by which they could play.

"I will be using the same game plan that I use for real, so you must swear that this will not be talked about after you leave here."

Paulo readily agreed, almost panting at the thought of having sex with these two hot guys.

"Ok, we'll go to the study. Your crime will be that you insulted a lecturer which rates the second level of punishment. Peter will be my senior witness and I will give him a little more leeway than I would in a real situation. If you enjoy tonight, we can go to the next level tomorrow which involves penetration."

Paulo's eyes were out on organ stops.

"Oh gosh, I didn't know you could go that far."

"Yes, and there is talk from the committee that I have to devise even worse punishments for the small hard-core and repeat offenders."

Jarek was sitting at his desk when Peter walked in escorting Paulo.

"For your insulting behaviour to a lecturer, I am going to instigate the second level of punishment. If you refuse to answer any question truthfully and I find out, or you balk at any order I give you, I will simply increase the punishment. And if I get an outright refusal, I will send for security and you will be taken away to serve a year in confinement. Do you understand?"

Paulo said he did, turning over in his brain the implications if he was ever a real offender.

"Very well, my supervisor will now strip you, and orders he gives you to facilitate that action are to be obeyed the same as if I was giving it. Go ahead now, Mr. Chambers."

Peter loved this part. Paulo was dressed casually, just wearing a shirt, T-shirt, trousers, and underpants with socks on his feet. Peter stood in front of Paulo, smiling. He undid the buttons on Paulo's shirt and removed it. The T-shirt came next and Peter casually ran his hands over the exposed torso, particularly the nipples. He then dropped to his knees, gave Paulo permission to keep his balance by holding on to his shoulders and then to lift his feet one at a time to remove his socks. Peter could see that Paulo was already excited by the size of the bulge in his trousers. He undid his trouser belt, unclipped the top of his trousers and slid them over his hips, letting them drop to the floor. Peter gulped at the size of the erection that he could see through the underwear. He lifted the waist band over the cock and pulled them down, ordering Paulo to step out of them before he stood up to the side so that Jarek could see Paulo's cock as well. They both gulped. It was huge. It was standing up almost hugging his stomach and Jarek's first assessment was that it would measure twelve inches. Then he recalculated because he was looking at it from the underside.

"Very impressive and how long is it?"

Paulo was blushing but replied in a firm voice, "It's 26 centimetres, Sir."

Quick calculation and Jarek came up with a little over 10 inches.

"I think you should check out the area, Mr. Chambers."

Peter had a good feel around, front, and back. Paulo had a gorgeous butt as well as a fantastic cock. He so wanted to get down on it and hopefully take it in his arse at some time this weekend. Jarek let him play for a few minutes, giving him the opportunity to fondle the balls and wank the cock for a while.

"Mr. Chambers has been far too considerate with you so I think you should undress him and show your appreciation by giving him a first class blowjob."

Paulo was so keen to see Peter naked and erect he didn't finesse the strip at all. When Peter was naked and standing with his legs spread quite wide, Paulo was on his knees playing. He licked Peter's cock and balls while he explored his back end. He worried Peter's anal entry without actually penetrating him, but it was exciting enough for Peter to get even harder. He sat down in an armchair after a few minutes and let Paulo get on with it. The boy was patently very experienced or had worked out what would turn himself on the most and just did it to Peter. Even Jarek had never given him a blowjob as good as Paulo. His orgasm was quite spectacular and Jarek could see how many jets of cum Peter pumped into Paulo's mouth. Sitting back and panting afterwards, Peter turned to Jarek and spoke, "You've got to have one of those, Babe. This guy is a marvel, the best blowjob ever."

Jarek laughed.

"In that case why not. Paulo, you can undress me and I'll accept a repeat performance. If it isn't the best blowjob, we will have to punish you even more in the morning."

Peter had been correct and the resulting orgasm was incredible. But Jarek had an evil grin spread across his face as he gave his verdict.

"Humph, not very good at all so we will continue this punishment session tomorrow and we will see if your other end is any better."

Both younger men looked with shock at Jarek and then saw his wicked grin. Paulo thought it was marvellous and responded, "Oh yes, Sir. This miserable individual will try even harder to please you tomorrow."

Grown men giggling could sound ridiculous, but these three appeared to add so much humour to the giggles that it was funny.

"Come along then, let's see if I can find a night cap for us. I don't think we need worry about dressing again."

There were three very contented young men who fell into bed that night, with Paulo in the middle of the other two.

"We couldn't possibly let you sleep by yourself after giving us such fine entertainment."

That was how Jarek decided the sleeping arrangements. Peter was delighted because it was he who had to spoon into Paulo, going to sleep with that enormous cock lodged in his crack.

The next morning came with a very decorous start. Everyone showered and just donned briefs before sitting down to breakfast.

"We know where we are going with this Paulo so we'll forgo CDO role-playing if you like. We can either resume in an aggressive mode in my study, or we can turn it into a love in, in our bedroom."

Paulo, with laughter in his voice replied, "Oh, I would love you to be the aggressive and sadistic CDO."

Jarek looked at Peter and grinned.

"Well, I've never been sadistic in my punishments but I can certainly try this morning."

Breakfast completed and Paulo was standing in front of Jarek's desk, naked again.

"Our little import doesn't take this seriously enough, Peter, so I think we need to ginger him up a little."

Jarek moved from behind his desk and knelt down in front of Paulo.

"I don't like punishing excessively hairy guys so I think we will do some trimming first. Paulo, lie on my desk on your back."

Peter was fascinated as he watched Jarek. He moved Paulo's cock so that it lay up his tummy, then he took the balls in his hand and started pulling the hairs out. It looked really painful but in reality, it was incredibly erotic and Paulo was soon erect as he leaned on his elbows to watch Jarek. It took quite a while but eventually, Jarek stood back grinning. Paulo didn't have a hair on his balls and it looked so sexy. Jarek asked Peter if he wanted to do the tongue test on them. That was no contest. Peter had both of them in his mouth, slathering them. Jarek left the study while that was going on and came back with a razor and shaving oil. Peter stood back then and Paulo held his breath, thinking he was going to lose his pubic hair. He ended up with a very neat trimmed patch.

"Roll over now, boy, come up on your knees and spread your legs as wide as you can. Peter, you go round the other side of the desk and pull his cheeks apart so that I can shave the hair in his crack."

This was becoming more erotic by the minute. Jarek was working through some of his fantasies and some of the things he was going to introduce as more extreme punishments as CDO. Shaving finished and Peter was ordered to move his hands in a little closer so that he could spread the cheeks more. Paulo was told to drop his head and shoulders onto the desk. Peter watched Jarek slick up three fingers with loads of spit before easing the first one over Paulo's sphincter. Soon, another followed and he started rotating them.

*'Oh God, please let me do that,'* was Peter's thought and almost on cue, Jarek told him to change places. All three young men were almost peeing pre-cum. Jarek and Peter eventually took their briefs off.

For the next quarter of an hour or so, Peter and Jarek finger-fucked Paulo, increasing the number of fingers they were using. After Paulo had orgasmed twice, Jarek made him get off the desk and bend over it with his feet astride. He took some gel from a desk drawer and coated Peter's cock in it before sliding some into Paulo.

"This dirty boy keeps ejaculating so you should help his next one by fucking him."

Peter loved it. He entered Paulo slowly and then fucked him with long strokes, using his hands to play with a very hard, long cock and stroke the remainder of the body that he could reach. He was so turned on that he only lasted about ten minutes, and that was a struggle. His orgasm was quite violent and he went soft quickly after it before sliding out of Paulo's welcoming arse. Jarek slid in straightaway and disgraced himself, cumming in under two minutes.

"I'm sorry, Paulo, I couldn't last any longer. You are just so incredibly sexy. You can punish me if you like by fucking me."

Paulo didn't need telling twice. He had Jarek on his desk in the missionary position and entered him with just lube on his cock, forgetting to open Jarek up first. The entry was painful, but very quickly Jarek was flying high feeling sensations in his insides that he never had before. Not surprising really, ten inches and thick would have any anus crying for more. The prostate took so much punishment that Jarek came at least four times. It might have been more as the orgasms were so close together. Paulo's orgasm was his most intense ever. He had never fucked another guy before.

Peter was so turned on he had cum again then used loads of tissue to do a quick clean up on the others before they all crashed out on the chairs.

"I think we should continue Paulo's punishment when he has recovered by making him fuck you as well, Peter."

Peter beamed and said, "Yes, please."

That was the finale of the first morning session. Paulo took Peter round the planets, giving him fantastic orgasms the same as he had done for Jarek.

After everyone showered and dressed, they sat in the lounge with lunchtime drinks and Jarek summed it up.

"I know I'm going to love you and live with you for as long as you will have me, Peter, but do you think we could move Paulo in as our resident sex god?"

Peter laughed and replied, "Oh yes, please."

Giggles again before Jarek got serious.

"I'm pretty certain I'm speaking for Peter as well, Paulo. If you want to stay any time that we are not committed to other things, you will be very welcome. Role-playing has been fun. If you come again, we can make you the CDO and possibly even broaden the punishments depending on your imagination. Peter and I have indulged in fairly conventional sex because we love each other so much, but broadening our education can be fun. It will always be consensual so I am not suggesting that we will ever go for bondage, but we might get a lot kinkier if we all like it."

That was obviously a popular suggestion as Paulo and Peter both applauded with broad grins on their faces. Jarek kept making it even better for Paulo.

"Provided you have never been before me for punishment, Paulo, I will ask you to be one of my witness seniors next college year."

Paulo was delighted. He could just imagine how much sex he was likely to get, or at least witness.

The afternoon was spent lazing around, talking about college, and Paulo's expectations for the future. He stayed for dinner again and then left early.

"I have a heavy schedule on Mondays so I need to spend tomorrow studying and getting my assignments out of the way to start the week clean. Thank you both for an amazing weekend. I promise not to bug you too often but I would like to repeat what we have done this weekend."

"You are very welcome and we would as well. Talk to me during the week and we may be able to do this next weekend."

After Paulo had gone, Jarek got serious with Peter.

"Are you sure you want to do that again, Lover."

"Oh yes, if you do as well. He is such a sexy guy and that cock is to die for. I love you so much but I have to admit, bringing someone else into our sex life is very stimulating. Will you just fuck me here? No finesse, just shove your cock into me."

Happy to oblige and then it was time for bed.

Paulo did join Jarek and Peter for sex most weekends until the end of term. Jarek released all of his seniors from witness duty and advertised on the school notice board for replacements. He selected the six he needed and two extras as spares in case any balked at his introduction which was the same as last time. He was more experienced now and tried to pick guys that were either gay or bi. Two of them made it easy by bowing out, too straight to want to play with other guys.

One of the successful ones was Paulo who grinned like an idiot as the other boys gasped at the size of his cock when they stripped and played with themselves. Jarek hoped that Paulo plus one other would be able to replace Marcus and Jack who were both seniors and whom he had released from duty. Marcus reluctantly said, "Please, Sir, I can still do this as well."

Jarek laughed, "Cock hound, I would love to keep you until you leave, but the regulations forbid it. You'll have to apply to become a CDO as soon as you graduate. The program starts in earnest over the summer."

Jarek didn't think a new graduate would be accepted. Particularly as psychology graduates would almost certainly be preferred. What he didn't know was that Marcus had done psychology as a separate module, not getting as far as Jarek had done, but still a possible candidate.

By the end of term, the new boys had done very little. Jarek had them all in to his office before college closed for the summer and briefed them.

"I know you have not had much action these last few weeks but I can promise you that during the first half of term, you will get plenty as the new intake of freshmen will try it on to see how far we can go."

Paulo moved in with Jarek and Peter for the summer, but settled in to the spare bedroom.

"We love having sex with you, Paulo, but we need quality time together sometimes as well."

Paulo beamed.

"Thank you, Jarek and Peter. I am just so happy that I will have a beautiful home to live in for the summer, and two very sexy men who will allow me to play sometimes."

Jarek gave Peter permission to have private sex with Paulo because he was going to spend so much time at the new training centre for CDOs and with the committee. His first year results meant that the original 50 new CDOs had grown and there would be as many as they could recruit whom Jarek thought would need minimum supervision. The course would need to be longer and more intense. Role-playing was considered and then had to be thrown out in favour of more exposure to Jarek's DVDs from his first year, including the most extreme and the ones involving girls. The ones with Sheila in were worth their weight in gold.

When Jarek started on the final batch of new trainees, he was informed that he needed to choose a deputy from this intake. So, if one of the new graduates who were all less qualified than they wanted had potential, it would be a good move because he could be more closely supervised. Jarek knew who he was going to choose as soon as he looked among the young and eager faces. Marcus had the widest grin of all, with Jarek being a close second.

"Good morning, gentlemen. It has been decided that one of you will be my deputy and therefore, will get an easy ride on this course because he will be supervised by me at college. This is not a competition because I have already chosen him. He was one of my senior supervisors at my college in the first year of the program. Marcus, please come to the front. I am going to use you to help me with the remainder."

Marcus was delighted. He had genuine deep affection for Jarek. The year, as one of his supervisors had been a fantastic experience, was full of fun and good sex. The best of all had been fucking Peter. He hoped that he would be able to renew that relationship if his lover had left the scene, still not aware that the lover was Jarek.

Training course finished with just two weeks to go before the new college year started. Jarek needed that time to rest. He was quite drained from the intensity of the course. He also expected to be consulted frequently by new CDOs who were not sure how to tackle some problems. He expected to spend a lot of time either video conferencing with actual situations, or talking on the telephone. The day before the whole program became active again, the committee chairman called Jarek.

"We have been discussing the memo sent to you by the dean. We would like you to trial CDO involvement in the punishment sessions and report to us at the end of this term on how it has affected the overall program before we allow it as a general rule."

Jarek was over the moon. Now, the really cute ones would feel his cock. He needed to sit Peter down to talk that one through.

"Ooh, I like that. Will you make me a supervisor at the end of this year so that I can watch you perform with freshmen? I promise not to bankrupt you with my use of tissues to absorb all my orgasms."

Jarek sighed. He was so pleased that it didn't look as though this new sexual outlet was going to cause any problems. On past experience, it would probably enhance their sex life. Including Paulo in their sex sometimes had certainly made their private sessions incredibly erotic and satisfying.

# Chapter 9

"Peter, I have second year students as supervisors already so I don't see why you shouldn't be one as well. The only problem is that you are supposed to have a clean record to qualify and yours is a long way off that. I'll work on it and maybe ask the committee for a one off dispensation. I'll try to think of some good excuse. The fact that you are a psychology major may help because I can always say that I see in you CDO potential."

Peter grinned. The grin got wider a few weeks later when Peter was summoned officially to the CDOs office.

"Come in, Peter. We are just waiting for my two senior supervisors. You are in so much trouble again, I don't know how far I can go to punish you."

Peter looked bemused and tried to think of anything he had done wrong. He couldn't.

"I don't understand. I can't think of anything I have done wrong."

Jarek grinned then.

"I'm so pleased because it is actually Marcus I have sent for. He is going to take you through the responsibilities and duties of a supervisor. Your dispensation came through this morning. I'm going to give you the choice of turning it down though, because if you screw up at all as a supervisor your punishment will be far worse than any I have yet sanctioned."

Peter thought about that.

"No. I'm ok, Jarek. I won't screw up again."

Marcus came in then and was delighted to see Peter.

Jarek told him what he wanted.

"You can use my office. I'm going to be in a meeting with Annette for the remainder of the morning."

Jarek had been given a new office, detached from the college premises and Marcus had the old offices.

"Am I allowed to make this a practical briefing as well, Jarek?"

Jarek looked at Peter and grinned.

"I think that decision has to be Peter's."

Peter was shocked. Did Jarek mean he could if he wanted to? He definitely wanted to. He would love to feel Marcus reaming out his arse again, or him giving Marcus a blowjob. He decided finally to go the route they had discussed and invited Marcus to the flat in the same way that they had Paulo. Maybe he'd ask Jarek to make it a foursome with Paulo, which would be so erotic.

The briefing was comprehensive but Peter wouldn't let Marcus get practical, except the first stage. He thought it would be a tease to let Marcus see him naked and erect.

"I could, of course, order you to do the actions I specify. I am after all, deputy CDO."

"Yes, I know. Jarek has told me quite a lot already, but you have to wait if you want it to get practical to see if Jarek would approve when I tell him."

"Why would he worry?"

Peter moved in close and stroked Marcus' cheek, looking him in the eyes.

"Because, you remember I told you I wouldn't go to bed with you when you were a student because of my lover?"

"Yes. So?"

"Jarek is my lover, and has been almost from my first day here."

Marcus was so surprised he just looked at Peter and, "You lucky bugger."

He moved back and scoped out Peter's naked body and erect penis.

"I think so as well," Peter said, watching Marcus' eyes, "You can come to dinner one evening now that you are a staff. I'll talk to Jarek about it."

Marcus nodded and looked into Peter's eyes.

"You are such an incredibly sexy guy. I hope one day I will be able to fuck you again." He laughed then. "I would like to fuck you and have your boyfriend fuck me. What a tangled web human emotions make."

They both laughed and that was it. Peter was now looking forward to his first session as a witness and hopefully, participant to a punishment.

That night, curled up on the sofa, Peter told him about Marcus.

"Weird isn't it? He wants to be active with me and passive with you."

"That's easier than Paulo who likes to be both with both of us."

Another excuse for laughter before Jarek spoke, "We can invite him to dinner and a romp if you like. You can watch me fuck him and I can watch him fuck you, only I guess it will have to be lovemaking in both cases."

The deed was effectively done after that comment because both guys wanted it.

Being promiscuous would ruin most relationships, but because these two always did it together, well, apart from the holidays when Jarek was away, it appeared to have the opposite effect on them.

Punishment sessions were now run by Marcus with Jarek always in attendance to watch how he handled things. Jarek loved the first one where Peter was in attendance because Marcus favoured Peter. The boy concerned was a freshman who had achieved college entry standard, but only just, because he was a rabble-rouser.

Marcus had attended enough of these with Jarek to be word perfect. The boy was Joel Parkins and Marcus asked Peter to undress him. It was only achieved after two extra punishments were added. Jarek realized that this boy was a very slow learner. He did understand the bit about going to jail but each time he refused to do something, he gave in when Marcus picked up the phone.

"I will give you one final reminder concerning your position, Mr. Parkins. To date, your extras include being brought to an erect state, made to wank yourself to orgasm, and finally to give Mr. Chambers a blowjob to orgasm swallowing all his sperm. If you clock up any more, the next one will give myself or Mr. Howard the pleasure of fucking you to orgasm. I can build the punishment beyond that which will, I am sure, please Mr. Chambers and myself."

Peter was taking all this in. He hoped the guy would continue to dig his own grave. He would love to see Marcus' giant killer ream out this arrogant shit, even if he did have a fabulous cock.

Joel looked very unhappy. While he thought about it he did manage to orgasm, albeit a rather weak one.

"Now Mr. Parkins, show as much finesse as you can in undressing Mr. Chambers. And using your hands, get him an erection."

Again, he carried out the order.

"Very good, Peter, make yourself comfortable in a chair on the platform. Mr. Parkins, on your knees between his legs and show us what a great cocksucker you can be."

Joel stood back and almost screamed, "No fucking way."

Marcus picked up the telephone again and actually spoke to security, summoning them to the CDO's office.

"You will have one year to think about your actions after security removes you from here."

For the first time, security actually entered the CDO's office. Peter had been sent to the bathroom so that only Parkins remained, naked.

"No, don't let them take me, Sir. I'll cooperate now, I swear."

Marcus spoke to the security then, "Please, wait in the outer office for ten minutes, gentlemen. If you aren't called again by then, you can leave."

Peter returned to his comfortable position on the chair and Joel gave him a very poor blowjob that hadn't even made him orgasm after ten minutes. Marcus then ordered him onto the punishment table where he was strapped down completely. The stirrups were wound back until Joel was spread as wide as he could be and his knees were touching the bench on either side of his shoulders.

"You can demonstrate the art of cock sucking if you like, Peter, without actually letting him cum. You are to fuck him then to your own orgasm. Mr. Howard and I will follow you to complete the extra punishments."

Parkins looked shocked. He did get an incredibly sensuous blowjob from Peter but the latter pulled off before he could orgasm. The cock was a wonderful appendage with a neat ball sac. It was uncircumcised but the skin was fully retracted when it was erect. Peter had loved sucking it and playing with the balls. He loved it even more when he had lubed the two of them and slid his man rammer all the way in, in one smooth entry. Joel screamed like a stuffed pig until Peter stopped moving to give him time to adjust. Then, showing how professional he had become, practicing on Jarek, he fucked Joel to a very satisfactory orgasm, returning Joel to an erect state by punishing his prostate.

Marcus undressed next, but Jarek tapped him on the shoulder and whispered in his ear, "I am sure I will cum in my pants watching you fuck him. Let me go first."

Marcus sniggered, "Be my guest, Mr. Howard."

Peter loved it. Jarek only lasted a couple of minutes and then it was Marcus' turn. Peter was hard again as he watched one very substantial cock pistoning into a not so arrogant student, now.

Three satisfied disciplinarians and a considerably less arrogant student stood in front of them.

"Mr. Parkins, considering your obduracy, I think you have escaped lightly today. I don't know how good your imagination is but when you leave here, think about your next visit starting at this point and imagine what else we can do to make your life unbearable. You may now leave."

Jarek looked at his two naked compatriots and sniggered.

"Now that is what I call a punishment session. It makes this job worthwhile."

Peter and Marcus were almost falling over with laughter.

"Gentlemen, I think we should shower and resume normal duties."

The shower was fun with way too much groping and three more orgasms.

"Marcus, why don't you come to dinner tonight, perhaps, we can continue this action without Mr. Parkins being present."

Marcus and Peter exchanged glances. Marcus, almost panting at the thought, gulped out a yes.

"By the way, Marcus, I think you handled it perfectly. None of us expected it to go this far so I am delighted at the way you let the whole exercise flow."

Marcus glowed with the praise from his hero.

It had taken more than a year and at last, Jarek was going to get his hands on Marcus. He and Peter discussed the parameters they would work on that night.

"I want to fuck him. If that happens, shall we let him be the CDO and we'll be the naughty students? That guarantees you getting fucked by him and means I will probably get to blow him as well, while I wait to take him in my arse after you."

Peter was grinning.

"Lovely idea, if that works we could expand it next time and have Paulo here as well"

"Yes and speaking of Paulo, I haven't used him in a really raunchy punishment session yet. I must do so because I would like to see him using his appendage on a stroppy student."

"Me too, will you use us both together when it happens?"

Jarek laughed so hard he nearly wet his knickers.

"Can you imagine yourself and Paulo as student witnesses, Marcus as CDO, and me monitoring the session?"

Thought spoken, it was bound to happen now.

The student who became the recipient of their plan was a wolf in sheep's clothing. Luke Atkins was a freshman at the lower end of the age bracket. He graduated from high school ahead of his peers and hadn't celebrated his eighteenth birthday until after half-term, when most of his classmates had recognized the need to behave. The ones that had graced Jarek's rooms became good boys and their friends had been told why. Luke must have either been deaf, unbelieving, stupid, or a complete sucker for punishment and humiliation.

The problem with the really clever ones was that they frequently thought they knew more than their professors. Luke had gotten into a serious slanging match that ended with him pushing the professor. Marcus had sent the details to Jarek because it was a category three offence. The law had been tightened up to protect teachers and lecturers from aggressive students, so in a criminal court it was an offence warranting imprisonment. Jarek had pulled up the boy's stats and photo before actually seeing him.

*'My God, the boy is an angel sent down to earth to torment people like me,'* was Jarek's thought as he looked at the picture. He didn't want to punish this boy. Instead, he wanted to take him to bed and

make love to him forever. *'That is no doubt what he has relied on all his life,'* was his next thought. He walked over to the CDO's rooms and passed Luke secured to a chair in the outer office. The boy's look was truculent but he still caused a serious stirring in Jarek's groin. Marcus looked up as Jarek walked in. The look was anguished.

"What are we going to do to him? I want to take him to bed and make love to him forever, never mind punishing him."

Jarek nodded, "Let me see the lecturer's report."

Marcus passed it across with a doleful look on his face.

"I can't see any mitigating circumstances."

After reading the report, Jarek couldn't either.

"I'm going to get his side of the story. I'll record it for you to transpose for your records. This may well be a case that you can use as a template. We seldom have category 3 punishments to render."

Jarek took the report with him and sat next to Luke, both of them turned in their seats to scrutinize each other.

"You know who I am, Luke?"

"Yes, Sir, you're the director of disciplinary officers. The head honcho."

"Correct, and you know there is a CDO who normally handles discipline in this college?"

Luke nodded.

"Do you know why I am involved this time?"

Luke had all of a sudden lost his tongue, but he nodded.

"Tell me."

Beginning to look worried he replied, "Because I physically abused a staff member."

"Precisely, and your reply confirms my opinion of you. You used exactly the terminology that will go into my report. Read this and tell me if it is a true statement of the events."

Jarek handed him the professor's report.

Looking less happy by the minute, Luke handed it back to Jarek.

"That is correct, Sir, but it sounds worse than it really was, written down."

"You did push the professor hard enough for him to hit the wall, to stop him from falling over?"

A very soft, "Yes, Sir," confirmed the only thing that really mattered.

"I have checked your stats. You are a first class student, you play Lacrosse at county level and you come from a background that most boys would give their souls for. What on earth possessed you to do this?"

The temper showed then.

"The man's an idiot."

"The man has a PhD, a doctor and professor of many years standing. I doubt he is an idiot."

Luke just looked belligerent but didn't say anything else.

"I'm sorry, Luke. I have no choice but to sanction our most severe punishment, or have you sent for a criminal trial. You may get away with just one year as it was a minor assault. If you opt for CDO punishment it will be the most humiliating we can give you involving the full gamut of gay sex, followed by a paddling that will keep you sore for weeks. I am giving you the choice."

"Your punishment, Sir," came back very fast.

"Very well but be warned, if you balk at anything you are asked to do, you will be taken away to a police cell."

Luke looked worried and that got worse as Jarek continued, "Have you ever given a blowjob, or received a penis in your anus?"

Luke looked shocked.

"No, neither, Sir."

"Well, you need to psyche yourself for that because you will no doubt give several blowjobs and receive as many penises in your anus."

"You can't do that. That's vile and disgusting."

"I can, and much more if I want to. There are virtually no limits to what CDOs can do in the way of humiliation and punishment."

Luke looked seriously worried.

"I will leave you to think about this while the CDO gets his two student witnesses organized."

Luke knew from others that there were always two students who witness the punishment. That thought made him cringe.

Jarek went back to Marcus.

"I think you had better see if you can get Peter and Paulo for this one. You know how to carry out a cat 3 punishment don't you?"

Marcus nodded. They had joked about doing one but now that it was going to be a reality, they weren't so happy. That might have had something to do with the boy outside waiting for it. *'He's too beautiful to abuse,'* was the thought of both CDOs.

Lecture conflicts meant that they couldn't get witnesses until the end of lectures.

Jarek was going to release the boy and hoped that he ran away. Let the police handle it then.

"I am going to release you to your lectures for the remainder of the day. When you finish for the day, I want you to go back to your dorm, give yourself a couple of douches and have a shower. You are to be here not later than thirty minutes after your last lecture, dressed in shorts and T-shirt. Do you understand?"

Jarek released him as he replied, "Yes, Sir."

Back with Marcus, and Jarek briefed him.

"I want you to start with as many embarrassing questions as you can, make him squirm a little, but that is after he is naked. Make Peter and Paulo undress him. He must have an erect penis after that, use any means you like then get him to blow the two boys. From there you can get a blowjob if you want to and then all three of you fuck him, make it as humiliating as you can. Finally, give ten with the paddle. It should've been twenty but I don't want to destroy him."

Marcus agreed, so Jarek went back to his own office, very unhappy for the first time since he took this job.

He arrived back at the CDO's office at the same time as Peter and Paulo.

When Marcus had finished briefing them, Peter was almost drooling.

"Oh my God, I have seen the guy round campus. He is the most stunning human being I have ever seen."

No argument there.

# Chapter 10

Luke arrived on time and was immediately brought in and made to stand on the platform. Marcus appraised him of the situation as had Jarek earlier.

"Any dissent and we add more punishments until we run out of ideas when we call the police. Understood?"

A very unhappy student nodded his head.

"Verbal acknowledgement please, Mr. Atkins."

"I understand your briefing, Sir."

"Very well, my two student supervisors will undress you. Obey them the same as you would me."

When Luke was naked, he was told to play with himself and get an erection. The boy was an obvious athlete with a lightly muscled body. His erect penis was uncut with a good length and thickness, sitting above a very pretty ball sac. A head of unruly, dark brown hair topped off the image with the most beautiful, intelligent-looking blue eyes below it.

"Peter and Paulo, I think you should both have a good feel of Mr. Atkins' body to make sure it is real."

Peter and Paulo thought so as well.

Peter had tears in his eyes while stroking Luke. He whispered in his ear, "I think you are the most beautiful creature I have ever set eyes on. I am so sorry that I am going to have to abuse your body."

Luke looked quite shocked and stared hard at Peter to see if he meant it. Conclusion, which flustered him, was that Peter was genuine in his statement.

A few minutes during which Paulo and Peter had felt every square inch of the boy they knew they were going to fuck, they were both as hard as they had ever been. Luke had elongated but was not yet erect.

"Thank you, guys. You can stand back now, while Mr. Atkins answers some questions. When did you last masturbate, Luke?"

Luke was thrown by the question and the use of his first name.

"Oh, er, this morning."

"And how often do you do that?"

Luke blushed, "2 or 3 times a day."

"So, would you consider yourself oversexed?"

The smile as Luke replied made Peter's look of anguish surprise Jarek, who was watching.

"No, Sir. I think I'm quite normal."

"Normal with boys or normal with girls?"

Luke blushed, "With girls, Sir."

Luke knew that to be a lie. He thought he would be normal with girls, but he had no experience apart from some juvenile fumbling the same as with boys.

"That's a pity," said Jarek, "Because when you leave here today you are going to have a huge amount of experience with boys."

Peter and Luke both winced.

"Have you ever played sex games with boys?" was Marcus' next question.

Luke wanted to say no, but most boys did a little boy-boy experimentation so he admitted to it.

"Have you ever blown a boy?"

Rapid shake of the head before a very positive, "No," came out.

"Very well, now play with yourself and let us all see an erect penis."

Luke shook his head. No sound came out but the look on his face was agony.

"Very well, I'm adding one more punishment and, Peter, do the job for us."

Peter faced Luke so that no one else could see his face. He spoke very quietly as he started to fondle Luke's cock and balls, "Please, do everything you are asked. The extra punishments will be quite horrendous for a straight boy. I would kill for an opportunity to make love to you, but I am not going to enjoy abusing you."

Luke looked closely at Peter and could see the anguish on his face and the tears in his eyes. He didn't know what to think. Peter was so cute and looked so innocent. He nodded. "I'll try."

Peter played beyond the getting hard stage, making Luke feel more excited than he ever had before.

"You are so exciting touching me, Peter. I might like you going further."

Peter was shocked, shook his head, and stepped back.

"Well done, Peter. Luke you can now undress Paulo. Let him get comfortable in a chair and then Peter will talk you through the best method of sucking and making him orgasm in your mouth. You will of course, swallow all of the sperm or we will start adding extra strokes to your punishment."

When Luke saw how huge Paulo was, he gulped. Knelt between his legs, Luke looked at Peter who had knelt beside Paulo so that the two CDOs could see all the activity.

Speaking quietly and gently, Peter started giving Luke instructions. He learned how to caress Paulo's cock and balls with spit-slicked hands as well as lick and suck on the glans. With Paulo's cock lying across his belly, Luke licked up and down the underside. He tickled behind the balls, let a hand run up to and play with the nipples. Paulo thought that if Peter was this good at instructing, he must be sensational with Jarek, whom he loved. The resulting orgasm when it came was sensational and nearly choked Luke.

"Swallow it all, Luke."

He didn't really have any choice as Paulo kept holding him onto his cock. Luke kept sucking until Paulo let him free.

"Thank you, Peter. I'll bring all my future boyfriends to you for training. That was quite a sensational blowjob."

He patted Luke's head as he was speaking.

Marcus piped up then.

"Well done, Luke. Why don't you undress Peter and show him how good his instructions had been."

Peter was delighted with the quality of the blowjob. He was stroking Luke's hair and whispering words of encouragement to him all the way through. Luke looked up into Peter's face several times during the action and was surprised to see a look he didn't understand, but it had a softness about it that both pleased and confused him.

The downside for Luke was that each action was so humiliating. The humiliation appeared to expand so that when he was made to blow Marcus, he wanted to cry.

"I will take the third slot, Luke, to check your progress."

This third one wasn't as good and Marcus guessed why. He and Jarek had swapped glances as they watched Peter and Luke reacting to one another.

Jarek was praying that Luke wasn't gay.

The punishment bench was next and Luke blushed over most of his body when he was positioned with the stirrups, as wide and far back as they could be without breaking his back or splitting him in two. The four men standing at the end of the bench looking straight down at Luke's body had never carried such monstrously hard cocks.

"Peter, you and Paulo can open him up and you can take the first fuck."

Peter wanted to say no. He used gel from the start, which was unusual, but meant that even the first finger would go in without any pain. He ran a finger around the anus just gently sliding over it occasionally. Then he put pressure on the entrance and whispered to Luke, "Please, try to relax. I can do this with no pain but not if you tense up."

Luke nodded, saw how much Peter cared and did as he was asked. The others then started to move around watching, which ramped up the embarrassment and humiliation until Peter lubed his cock and slid it over Luke's sphincter without any spike of pain. A slow and very sensuous fuck followed until both young men orgasmed. Peter's experience once again, paid off. He had played with Luke to make sure that their orgasms were together.

Paulo, Marcus, and Jarek followed. Jarek was more aggressive than normal because he was sure Luke was going to cause a disruption in his relationship with Peter.

The session ended with Marcus delivering ten, quite hard swings of the paddle to Luke's arse, rendering considerable pain. After the punishment was completed, Jarek told Paulo and Marcus to shower while he just wiped himself clean.

"We are going to leave you to sort out Mr. Atkins, Peter."

Jarek then shuffled everyone else out.

Peter undid the strap around Luke's waist.

"Slide up onto the bench, Luke. I'm going to cream your bottom to take away some of the pain and bring the bruising out."

Peter had tears running down his face as he looked at the terribly bruised bottom. It was the most beautiful rear end he had ever seen and to him it was a terrible crime to have damaged it. He gently applied the soothing cream to it until he felt Luke relaxing and knew that the anaesthetic in it was working.

"Open your legs now, Luke. I'm going to do the same thing inside you. I will only use one finger."

Luke said nothing but was fully aware of how gentle Peter was to him and had been throughout. All finished and he turned over taking in Peter's face and gasping with shock. Peter was still crying silent tears.

"Why?"

Peter shook his head from side to side.

"You are so beautiful. I don't care what you did. I could never hurt you or embarrass you by choice."

"But you don't even know me."

"I don't care. I just think I love you."

Luke was really astounded.

"But I don't even think I'm gay."

"It doesn't matter. Please be my friend, Luke. Give me a lifetime to make amends for this afternoon."

Luke touched Peter's face.

"I'm blown away. I don't know what to say. I'm really not a very nice person so I will have to change an awful lot to be worthy of your love."

Peter smiled through his tears.

"Does that mean we can both try?"

Luke nodded shyly.

"I think I would like that."

"If you have a shower now, I'll cream your bottom again before you dress. I won't have to do inside," and he smiled.

Before Luke left, they exchanged cell numbers and Peter kissed Luke quickly and softly on the lips.

"We will talk again, soon."

Luke nodded.

When Peter walked into the apartment, Jarek tried to sound unconcerned.

"Everything cleared up ok?"

Peter nodded, "Yes, I creamed his bottom and let him shower before I showed him out, and then I showered there as well."

Jarek could still see that Peter had been crying.

"Come and sit down. Do you want to talk about it?"

Peter shook his head.

"No, I need to straighten out my own head before I can talk to you."

Jarek looked worried. He had watched Peter's reaction throughout the punishment and it was worse than his when he had to punish Peter.

"Am I going to lose you?"

It was said with so much sorrow in his voice that Peter looked at his lover, almost in shock.

Peter disintegrated throwing himself into Jarek's arms.

"I don't know. Oh God, my love. I think I love him, but I don't even know him."

Peter was sobbing now, his thoughts in turmoil. What he had with Jarek was like nothing he had ever expected. The thought of ending it filled him with dread, but his feelings for Luke had been so strong almost from the second he set eyes on him.

For the first time ever, these two lovers didn't snuggle that night. Peter was almost rigid with the fear that Jarek would try to spoon him as normal. He didn't want any human contact while he sorted out his brain. It was a very tense and quiet breakfast the next morning. Peter left the flat as soon as he could. Sitting on a bench on campus, he called Luke and told him where he was.

"Can we talk before you go to your lectures?"

Luke was there five minutes later. They touched hands and looked into each other's eyes.

"I don't know what to do. For the first time ever, my boyfriend and I didn't cuddle last night. I can't get you out of my head and he is frightened I am going to leave him. He saw how I reacted to you yesterday."

"Oh, I didn't realize Paulo is your boyfriend."

Peter looked at him as though he was mad.

"Paulo is just a friend," he laughed.

Luke's eyes opened as wide as saucers.

"The CDO is your boyfriend?"

Shake of the head, "No, the Director."

Luke was patently shocked.

"Oh shit, I'm dead."

That made Peter laugh, "No, you aren't. You have no idea what a wonderful person he is. I love him so much, but you are turning my world on its head. I know the dean will hate me now as well, and he has been so good to me."

"What has the dean got to do with it?"

More surprises for Luke.

"Jarek is the dean's brother."

"Oh my God, I'm going to pack and get out of this college today."

Peter thought Luke was joking, and laughed until he saw the look.

"No Luke, that won't solve anything. Tom and Jarek will both act like grownups, but if you and I become lovers I know it will devastate Jarek and I don't want to hurt him."

"So what do we do?"

"I don't know. I guess we have to see as much of each other as we can, and we need to go to bed sometime to see if we make sweet music together."

"I might not want gay sex all the time, or even at all."

"If you don't want it at all, I guess we just become good friends."

They parted to go to their lectures, promising to meet for lunch. Their hands touched again and there were electric shocks that passed between them.

Peter had a miserable morning, but not as miserable as Jarek.

At lunchtime, Peter and Luke took sandwiches and sat out on the grass away from everyone else. They talked about each other's lives catching up on nearly 20 years of history. Their childhoods were remarkably similar and Peter wondered if that was why they had displayed such empathy for each other. Luke realized that he had felt the connection with Peter from the start, and that had almost certainly saved him more extra punishments. He knew that he had been a pain since coming to the college, displaying arrogance that he guessed was why he had not made any friends. Would he change now that he had someone he wanted to like, and maybe more? He knew about parental love, but the love that Peter was professing was a whole new world for him. *'I've probably been way to narcissistic,'* was his thought and that made him snigger.

Peter looked at him, "What?"

Luke touched Peter's arm. Peter gasped with the sensation of that innocent touch.

"I was thinking that the reason I have no friends here is because I have been arrogant, and also, I think I might be a little narcissistic. I promise I'm going to try to change. I want you to like me, Peter, even if it goes no further than that."

Peter's smile could have lit up the whole campus.

"I want that too. I want us to make love as well as soon as you feel ready for it."

Luke looked so serious now.

"I know that what you did to me was very thrilling even though I had no choice in the matter. My problem is that I am frightened to do it again even though I know you won't do anything I don't want."

Peter nodded. This long talk had made him feel easier in his mind. *'I think I can be normal with Jarek now and still progress my friendship with Luke. If we try sex and it is good for him then my problem is back, but until then I must convince Jarek that I will always love him whatever happens.'* With that thought, he and Luke parted for their afternoon lectures.

"Can we meet for lunch tomorrow as well?"

Luke smiled, "Yes please, same time."

Jarek looked worried when Peter walked into the flat at the end of his lectures. Peter went straight up to him and gave him an, 'I love you kiss,' making Jarek sigh.

"I don't know if anything is going to develop between Luke and me. I know I like him very much but beyond that, the only thing I can tell you is that I will always love you whether we are together or not."

Jarek knew he would worry while it sorted itself out, but there was nothing more that he could do. Dinner was a quiet affair but at bedtime, it was Peter who instigated sex, asking Jarek to make love to him. It was, as always, sensational loving.

# Chapter 11

The next day, Marcus and Jarek were sitting in Jarek's office discussing the punishment log and dissecting each one for the benefit of Marcus. When they broke for coffee, Marcus asked about Peter. Jarek knew what he meant. They had both noticed Peter's immediate attraction to Luke.

"I don't know. We were fine last night but he has admitted that he is confused about his feelings for Luke. The two of them had an immediate affinity towards one another and I know they have talked since. Peter says that he will always love me even if we are not together. I think that is a prelude to him and Luke becoming lovers. I just don't know."

Marcus tried to lighten the atmosphere at the same time indicating to Jarek how he felt. When he was a student he had the hots for Peter but since becoming Jarek's deputy he realized that he was falling in love with his boss. The extra maturity and compassion that he brought to a job where it would be so easy to become cynical and uncaring affected him greatly.

"Forever is a long time, Jarek. You have been Peter's first love and guided him through the early times giving him confidence until now. He is definitely his own man. If he and Luke becomes an item, can I audition to be his replacement?"

Marcus tried to make it sound like a joke but that wasn't how it came out and it made him blush. Jarek looked at him, searching his face for the expression he wasn't expecting.

"Oh, crikey, you're serious, aren't you?"

Marcus tried to deny it but he just blushed more and sounded so guilty with his denials.

"How long, Marcus?"

Shaking his head Marcus replied, "I don't know. Working so closely with you, it just sort of came up on me in slow time. You are such a wonderful person. You genuinely care for people, and even when you are dishing out punishment you watch and make sure you don't traumatize the straight boys with gay sex. You are never brutal with physical punishment and despite having almost limitless power you never appear to get off on it."

Jarek wanted to lighten the atmosphere so he laughed.

"Of course, I get off on it, particularly when I have you, Peter, or Paulo taking part. You must be the three sexiest men in college."

*'Yeah right,'* thought Marcus, *'and Luke is the sexiest of the lot.'*

Jarek had done it again. Used his innate kindness to defuse a possible embarrassing episode for Marcus, but it did leave him with plenty of thoughts. He had always been turned on by Marcus and had enjoyed immensely sex with him, but always just for fun. His mind had never strayed from loving Peter. Now he had to think of it as a possibility.

The worst possible time for it to happen, while he was in a difficult situation with Peter, Jarek got a summons to the ministry for a brainstorming session with the committee. He knew it would be a two or three day affair. He was packing to leave when Peter came in from his lectures.

"Where are you going?"

Peter had all sorts of things going on in his head, first of which was that Jarek was leaving him.

"Summons from the ministry. It looks like a two or three day affair."

Trying not to sound devastated at his next pronouncement.

"With an empty flat, it will give you a chance to sort out your relationship with Luke."

He wouldn't look at Peter, and Peter didn't look at him. He did feel like shit knowing that Peter was going to take advantage of his absence.

"I'm sorry. I don't know what else to say."

"Don't say anything. I'll deliberately make sure I'm away for three nights, which should give you enough time to make up your mind on what you want. If you aren't here when I get back I won't embarrass you by chasing you."

Peter was gutted at the casual way Jarek said it and looked up to see the expression on his face. What he saw devastated him. Silent tears were coursing down Jarek's face like twin waterfalls. He pulled Jarek into his arms and hugged him.

"Oh God, I am so sorry. I love you so much. I never want to hurt you. I just don't know what to do."

Jarek pushed him away and finished his packing.

"Do what you have to do."

With that he picked up his valise and walked out.

Peter just fell to the floor and sobbed.

"What am I going to do? I love him so much, but Luke is consuming me."

Peter didn't notice the passing of time until he noticed it was dark outside. He looked at his watch, it was 8 o'clock. He had been lying there for nearly four hours. He got up, cleaned his face, and went to the kitchen to make himself a drink. His cell rang while he was at the breakfast bar drinking.

"Peter, we need to talk. I am going crazy thinking about you."

Peter sighed, "You had better come round to Jarek's flat. He has gone to London. He'll be gone a few days."

Luke gasped. Took down the address and told Peter he would be there in ten minutes.

It was quite obvious when he arrived that he had come as he was: athletic shorts, T-shirt, and flip flops.

Peter gasped at the sight and Luke blushed.

"I'm sorry. I had just showered so I didn't bother to dress properly."

They went to the kitchen and Peter made Luke a drink. They sat opposite each other at the breakfast bar just looking at each other.

"I'm sorry to barge in like this but I have been tormenting myself thinking of you. I know you love Jarek but I think we need to find out what our relationship is going to be. Please, Peter, take me to bed and make love to me properly."

Peter gulped. Was this going to be the decider on his future with Jarek, or, more precisely, without Jarek.

"I have to shower first. I've only just got my act together after Jarek left."

They wandered through the bedroom and stood facing each other as they undressed. Of course, they had seen each other naked before, but this was different, this was so intimate. They scoped each other out for a minute before Peter turned and left for the bathroom. Over his shoulder he spoke to Luke, "You are still the most beautiful creature I have ever seen."

Shower completed and Peter walked back into the bedroom to find Luke still standing where he had been before. He took this apparition into his arms and kissed him. The kiss was a toe curler for both of them. Luke gasped.

"I never imagined it would be that sensational, Peter. Can we do it again?"

Peter kissed him again and thought he was going to die. He broke the kiss, took Luke's hand and led him to the bed. Luke just lay on his back looking at Peter propped up on one elbow. With his free hand, Peter started caressing Luke's torso. He leaned in for another kiss before his lips started following his hand. By the time he got to Luke's cock he was almost at overload. He couldn't let Luke touch him so he swivelled round, kneeling by the bed.

Giving Luke a blowjob was sensational. He played with the wonderful set of balls, swabbing them with his tongue as he tried to swallow them, stroking and wanking the cock at the same time. Then he started punishing the glans, making Luke gasp and stroke his hair.

"That is wonderful, Peter. No wonder they made me blow you as part of my punishment."

Very close to cumming now, Peter climbed back onto the bed in a 69 position.

"Slick up your fingers with spit, Luke, and then do everything to me that I do to you."

Peter started opening up Luke's anus. He was making it as erotic as he could because he wanted to keep Luke on the boil. When he was relaxed, Peter moved around. He lubricated Luke's cock and his own arse before sitting over Luke's penis. He lowered himself on to it making Luke's eyes almost pop out of his head. He took it all before fucking himself on it for a couple of minutes. The feeling was amazing. He lifted himself off, rolled to the side and told Luke.

"Now you take charge and fuck me to orgasm."

Luke moved between Peter's legs and Peter spread them wide and pulled them back. Luke's eyes were full of surprise and lust as he moved his monstrously hard cock to Peter's anal entry and then beyond, sliding it in until his balls were pressed against Peter's cheeks. The fuck was without finesse, just straight in and out until he came. Peter came as well, but that was because he was so horny rather than Luke's ability.

'It was his first one. I shouldn't expect it to be fantastic. I can teach him,' that thought stayed with Peter as they cuddled afterwards.

Luke recovered from an obviously intense orgasm and spoke to Peter looking up at the ceiling, "That was incredible for me, Peter, but I don't think it was for you. Will you fuck me next time? It was incredible for me when you did it before."

Peter rolled into Luke's arms and kissed him.

"It will get better as we get used to each other and you gain experience."

Luke could tell that Peter was disappointed so he was determined to do better. He knew that everything they had done tonight was exciting for him and he found it easy to accept that he was probably gay. Letting Peter fuck him again would confirm it one way or the other.

"We have at least two nights, Luke. Stay with me until Jarek gets back then we should know what we want to do with our relationship."

Luke thought that was a good idea. A quick shower and they were back to bed. Peter spooned into Luke, but it didn't feel right. They reversed and that didn't feel right to Peter either, but that was how they stayed.

Breakfast the next morning was uncomfortable before both went off to their lectures, agreeing to meet for lunch. Lunch was a tense hour and then it was back to the flat again at the end of the day. They showered together and played. Straight to bed and Peter made love to Luke, pulling out all the stops to make it sensational. It was for Luke, but not for Peter. They dined and a little later went back to bed. Luke made love to Peter this time and obviously enjoyed it, but Peter was once again disappointed.

'I want to love him because I think he is an incredible human being. But the fire that I still have when making love with Jarek isn't there.' That thought and the accompanying disappointment showed, making Luke sad.

"We aren't working are we, Peter? At least, not as we should."

Peter shook his head and the tears were barely contained.

"I think you are such an incredible person, but there isn't any fire."

"I hope you will still want to be my friend and will help me find a lover, because I know that what we have done together is very thrilling for me"

Peter let the tears slide down his cheeks and Luke wiped them away.

"I'm sorry, Peter."

"It's not your fault. I think our expectations were too high. I would love you to be my friend. I know I love you but not in the same way that I love Jarek. You are so amazing that I am sure when I advertise for a lover for you, it will take us months to sift through all the applicants."

Luke looked shocked and Peter dissolved in laughter.

"I was only kidding. But we will find you a lover."

Luke stayed the night again and they curled up together comfortably this time as friends. Breakfast was a jolly affair as they discussed the kind of lover Luke would like. Peter had two in mind already, Paulo and Marcus.

Peter had an evening by himself the next night thinking about Jarek. He had put him through an awful time while he sorted out his relationship with Luke. He knew he had much to make up to him. They had no contact this time while Jarek was away and Peter was beginning to realize what he might already have lost. He knew that he should expect Jarek to rail at him for his stupidity and cruelty. With that in mind, he went to see Marcus at lunchtime.

"I have been stupid and cruel while I suffered my infatuation with Luke. Will you lend me a punishment paddle? When Jarek gets back, I am going to insist that he punishes me for my stupidity. I love him so much and I've put him through hell."

Marcus looked at him and wanted the whole story. Peter reluctantly told him.

"I agree, you have been stupid and I'll lend you the paddle if you let me have Luke's cell number."

He grinned and Peter did as well.

"I told Luke I would help him find a boyfriend. I did think of you first and then Paulo."

"Good boy, write it on that pad on my desk while I get you the paddle."

Peter finished his lectures early and prayed that Jarek would be home today, but not before him. He was lucky he was home first then gave himself a couple of douches and showered before slipping on a pair of athletic shorts. He placed the paddle on the coffee table in the lounge then sat and waited. He heard the key in the door just after 5. He quickly slipped off his athletic shorts and stood in the centre of the floor, legs astride and hands at his side. Jarek walked in and stopped in shock. Peter threw himself to the floor, crawled to Jarek, and kissed both his feet. Then he crawled to the coffee table and picked up the paddle before returning to Jarek who was frozen in shock at his performance. Sitting up on his knees, Peter presented the paddle to Jarek and looked him in the eyes.

"I have been so stupid and caused you so much unnecessary pain that I deserve to receive a serious thrashing. I love you so much and know that I don't deserve your love, but please punish me and forgive me."

The tears were almost blinding Peter as he finished so he didn't realize that Jarek was crying as well.

He took the offered paddle, dropped to his knees to be at the same level as Peter, released the paddle and took Peter's face in his hands before leaning forward to kiss him.

"I love you as well. I told you I would, forever. I do forgive you and no, I won't punish you."

He stood up then pulled Peter to his feet and kissed him again. That kiss was a toe curler and quite involuntarily, Peter was as hard as he could ever remember, though he still dug his heels in over the punishment.

"You must punish me. I have truly been evil towards you, throwing your love in your face over my infatuation with another boy. If you don't, I will strike a lecturer so that you will then have no choice."

Jarek could see the determination.

"Please, Peter, I have to change. Have a think about this and let it go."

He walked through to the bedroom and changed into sweats. When he came back into the lounge Peter presented him with the paddle and then moved to stand behind one of the heavy chesterfield armchairs. He bent over it placing his hands on the seat, spreading his legs wide and straight. The back of the armchair was lower than the punishment bench in the CDO's office so his legs were out at a slighter angle and his butt was well up in the air. Any strokes to his buttocks would be downwards and automatically carry more power than the semi-sideways ones the bad boys took. Jarek was instantly erect looking at what was presented to him.

"Please Peter, no."

"You have to, ten hard ones. You must sear my brain with the pain so that I will never be this stupid again."

Jarek's shoulders sagged. He could tell that Peter wasn't going to give in.

"Very well, but you will count them and ask me for another one each time until I have delivered the ten. If the pain becomes too intense just give me the number but don't ask for another one."

Jarek crossed his fingers as he said that last bit hoping Peter would let him off with some of them. He looked at the boy's arse and thought how much he just wanted to slide his penis in there to give him pleasure. He delivered the first stroke using a medium amount of power. Peter gasped and then spoke, "One, may I have another?"

Each one after that elicited the correct response, but Jarek could hear the tension building after each one. He knew Peter was hurting. The cheeks were beginning to bruise already. The pain was increasing exponentially after each one despite Jarek trying to spread the strokes over different parts of the bottom. The problem with the paddle was that it was quite wide so that was not very successful. By seven, Peter was sobbing and hardly able to speak but he took the last three.

Jarek threw down the paddle and took Peter in his arms. The boy couldn't stand so Jarek carried him through to the bedroom and put him on the bed on his tummy. For the next half an hour, he was back and forth to the bathroom getting cold towels to take away the burning and to ease the pain. After that, he applied the cream that he used in the CDO's office. It was nearly three quarters of an hour before Peter stopped sobbing and turned his head to look at Jarek.

"I'm so sorry, please don't stop loving me."

Jarek shook his head. He slid onto the bed alongside Peter and took him in his arms

"I've told you I'm going to love you forever and I meant it. I could never stop loving you."

He pulled Peter's head towards him so that he could reach the lips that gave him such a thrill and kissed his lover's adorable lips.

"Now, no more of this silliness, how does your bottom feel?"

"Much better, thank you, I want to get up and help you with whatever you have to do before bedtime. I'll make up the bed in the other bedroom if you would like me to sleep there."

Jarek replied, "What I want you to do is to stop being silly or I will give you another ten with the paddle. I have told you I forgive you and I love you, no matter what you've done."

Peter realized he hadn't told Jarek what he had done, so he remedied that.

"I slept with Luke for two nights and let him fuck me, as well as me fucking him."

Jarek knew that this would probably happen but he was still shocked.

'He has taken his punishment. I mustn't let him know that I'm shocked,' he thought and then spoke, "So why aren't you with him now?"

"Because I realized that even after a year with you, there is nothing like the thrill that I have every time you and I make love. Luke and I are going to be friends and I'm going to help him find a boyfriend. What I felt for him was more than infatuation but less than love."

"Alright, Peter. I don't want this episode in our lives ever mentioned again. We are to behave as though it never happened."

Peter nodded his agreement, seeing the pain in Jarek's eyes. He slid off the bed, winced at the pain, but continued moving until he could face Jarek and kiss him again.

"I love you so much."

Dinner and early to bed, Peter on his tummy for the night, Jarek on his back thinking how close he had come to losing this boy whom he knew was his life.

# Chapter 12

Peter woke up the next morning with a warm feeling on his bottom. He looked around and noticed Jarek rubbing cream on his buttocks.

"Good morning, Peter, how are you feeling?"

Peter grinned.

"Better by the second," then he got serious, "I'm so sorry, my Love. Have you really forgiven me?"

Jarek leaned forward and kissed his boy.

"I'll always forgive you, but please try not to need it too often."

Peter still found it hard to believe how much Jarek loved him and the result was the tears coming. He whispered, "I won't. I can't believe I nearly ruined the best thing that has ever happened to me."

"Ok, that's enough now. Let's forget it. I'm home and we have some loving to make up. I'll have a busy day so let's have breakfast together and then I need to get to the office."

Peter hopped out of bed, gave Jarek a kiss, and headed for the shower. Jarek had been up for more than an hour, thinking about yesterday's events. He went out to the kitchen, poured himself a cup of coffee from the freshly made filter, and started making the scrambled eggs. He could hear the bacon sizzling under the grill so he pushed the toast down into the toaster and set the table. Peter walked in just as Jarek finished dishing up. He poured Peter a glass of juice and then sat opposite him.

"Don't think I'm going to do this for you every day. I just had lots of time after I woke up."

Peter didn't make the smart retort he had on the tip of his tongue. He just said a quiet 'thank you.'

It was a quiet day for both with no stress. Jarek's was spent mostly writing up notes on his two days of brainstorming with the committee. The new CDOs appeared to be handling things well. Reports were what Jarek expected and he only had to field a few calls from men not quite sure what to with some of the unusual disciplinary breaches.

The only problem now appeared to be the very few that had gone to cat 3 punishment but were being held over for more serious action. No one had imagined going beyond cat 3. Being made to blow another guy or guys and being fucked by them should have been enough for the hardest nut. What more could he recommend that didn't enter the realms of disgusting and kinky? Feedback from Marcus was one route and Paulo might be worth talking to. He came from one of the barrios in Rio where the police were known to commit awful deeds on the kids before killing them. What he did in the end was invite Marcus, Paulo, and Alec to join him and Peter for a drink at the flat the next night. Alec was invited, not because he was gay but because Jarek was sure he was a sadist.

"You are probably wondering why you're here. The answer is that I need some help. Bad boys and girls virtually never want to go beyond a cat 3 punishment, but a very few do. I need punishment that is more extreme than giving blowjobs, being butt-fucked, and paddled. I can't think of any so the floor is open to suggestions. Of course, everything said here is completely safe from being repeated outside, ok."

Everyone agreed and Alec started, "You could always piss on them or in them at both ends. Take pictures or videos of them being butt-fucked and giving head and then post them on the notice boards."

Jarek thought the picture suggestion had some merit but he loathed to implement the pissing thing.

"We could shave all of their pubic hair and make them walk around campus naked all day." That was Marcus and was a definite possibility if Tom would allow it.

"I like that, Marcus. I'll talk to Tom about that one. I'll consider your suggestions as well, Alec. What about you, Paulo?"

"I have watched the police double fuck a boy before shooting him in the head. I'm not suggesting we shoot anyone, but being double fucked is monumentally humiliating and painful. I have also watched gang bangs. You could invite several gay guys to a punishment session and let them all play with the arse of the miscreant before taking turns fucking him, or her."

"Yeah, I could go for that whatever the sex, an arse is an arse. My cock won't be able to tell the gender of the arse once it's buried deep." Alec was grinning as he said that and soon everyone else was as well.

"I like that, Alec. I'm sure a lot of the students will as well."

It looked as though in a very few minutes, Jarek had lots to work with. He went on his rounds and quizzed the students about how they like the new atmosphere in their college where students could study. Everyone loved it.

Jarek went to see Tom after lunch to talk about more extreme punishment.

"I know I can do what I am inclined to, Tom, but I am wondering if you will allow it in public. I have allowed punishment to be as degrading and embarrassing as I can, but still we have a few who appear to be able to take it. I want to be allowed to make the worst offenders attend lectures for a given period, naked and shaven of all hair except their heads. I also want it made clear that other students can further embarrass them while they are naked, both sexes. I don't see why girls should be treated less seriously and Annette agrees with me. Also, I think it is time for public punishment as well."

Tom was well aware that there was still a very small core of students that pushed their luck and struck lecturers or fellow students during lectures. He didn't want to see these students in prison. He wanted to see them graduate and take a useful place in society. Most of the abusive ones had come from abusive homes so it was difficult to dislodge the thinking from their brains. Prison wasn't the answer.

"Let's give it a trial for say, two weeks."

Jarek was delighted. He called on Marcus and after getting the restraint equipment out, he and Marcus played with it until they had wrist and ankle restraints adjusted so that a student with them on could walk ok, but not be able to kick someone. The wrist restraints had enough play for them to work but not to strike someone.

"We now have a cat 4 punishment. We go to cat 3 then shave them, and send them out onto the campus naked and restrained. Let it be generally known that their bodies can be explored while they are naked."

Marcus loved it.

"Now, let's go through the list and pick out the worse student. The other thing I am thinking of doing is make them drink urine and punish them in front of their lecture group. Make them give a blowjob and then keep the penis in their mouth while it pisses in them and on them."

Marcus was wide-eyed at the last bit.

"That's pretty disgusting, Jarek."

"I know, but what else can we do. Making them give blowjobs and take cock in their arses didn't appear to work with the few."

Luke Atkins topped the list. He had physically attacked another lecturer, same with his first offence. Marcus had him in the office and he was surprised to see just Marcus and two very burly security staff.

"You will have to be assessed for your mental state if you are ever brought before me again after we finish this punishment. Now, strip completely and put your shoes back on."

Luke thought that was amusing, but the smile left his face quite quickly when he felt the ankle restraints click into place limiting his leg movement. The two guards then fitted the wrist restraints. Marcus came round his desk with a plastic notice that he showed Luke first before securing it to his back.

The notice read, 'I am a serial abuser, please feel free to humiliate me in any way you desire.'

"You are to attend all of your lectures for the remainder of today. Now go."

Luke stood with his mouth open but no sound came out.

"If you aren't out of my sight in ten seconds you will receive ten with the paddle."

He went, accompanied by one security guard who had been briefed.

"You are to remain with him until the end of his lectures and then bring him back here."

Someone as gorgeous as Luke didn't even get to his first lecture before a group of girls blocked his way. Before they let him go, he was sporting a very hard cock. He was blushing as he took his seat. The student next to him had read the notice as he turned to sit.

"That looks interesting, Luke. You have a really cute butt. I'm going to love following you to your next lecture and playing with it."

Luke glared at him but didn't know what to say.

He had hands stroking his arse as he walked between lecture halls. The next lecture was being conducted by a professor who was friends with the one Luke had pushed.

"Mr Atkins, would you join me at the front of the class?"

Luke blushed as he walked down the steps to the front.

"Climb on to the table and face away from the class."

Luke daren't complain because he knew Jarek would find even worse punishments if he did.

"I hope you can all read the notice on Luke's back. Apparently, he found it so stimulating giving blowjobs and being butt-fucked at his last punishment session that even after receiving a paddling the lesson didn't go home. So, let's have some fun in this class and we'll continue lectures next time. If any of you would like to explore his body, please come down to the front."

For the next 20 minutes, he was kneeling on the table with students playing with his cock and fingering him. That was bad enough but before he was allowed to get down, he had to kneel with his legs as far apart as his restraints would allow and then fall forward so that his shoulders were on the table. His anus was now on display and two boys were summoned to spread his cheeks further.

"What you can see now is a receptacle that when enclosing your penises, boys, can give you splendid orgasms. We have time for a few of you to try it if you wish."

Luke was mortified. Six boys fucked him to orgasm. Because they all had substantial cocks they weren't shy shedding their clothes for the remainder of the class to see.

Taken back to the CDO at the end of lectures, he was asked if he would like another day of that. Of course, he wouldn't.

"If you are ever brought before me again, Luke, you will be used as a public urinal as well as what you experienced today."

That comment from Marcus effectively ended serious punishments at the college. Four more cat 4 punishments were carried out during the next month and then they died a natural death. During the next year only one cat 3 punishment was needed and Jarek thought his job was effectively at an end. CDOs became part-time jobs. Since most of them were psychology graduates, they spent most of their time giving lectures in their subject. A toned down version was started in high schools so that from eleven years old onwards students realized that schools were places of learning, and you did just that, or else.

Peter finished college and went into private practice as a psychologist, and Jarek remained at the college at which he had been

CDO, as a lecturer. Marcus moved to the ministry of education as director of the SDO and CDO program.

Luke Atkins! Well, he used his incredible good looks and his MBA to cut a swathe through the city as an investment advisor. He and Marcus became lovers and were regular guests at Jarek's and Peter's country house a short drive from college.

~~The End~~

Here is a sample from another story you may enjoy:

# Finding
# MICHAEL

GAY SUSPENSE

## Dexter Chase

"You have fouled your body on this infidel my son, but you have done it for the glory of Allah. Now we must make good on our promise to your grandfather and extract the most pain from his father before we dispatch the boy to join the other loathsome creatures of his race. You know what to do?"

"Yes Uncle. We have softened up the mother by sending her photographs of her beloved son as we have made his living conditions less and less palatable. The news is that she is making the father's life hell, as we planned. I have used the time to find ten of my warriors who have been endowed by Allah with the most incredible appendages. These men are truly awesome when naked and erect."

"Good, I wish to see the video before we send it to the she devil and her evil husband."

Abbas was his uncle's favourite nephew, and with no direct male offspring it meant that if he continued as he had done so far, he would inherit that uncle's wealth. The secret he would need to keep forever though was that he didn't consider he had fouled himself making love to this white boy, now languishing in squalid conditions in a hovel at the edge of the palace grounds. Abbas would suffer a terrible death if the uncle knew that he was a true homosexual and had not done it just to gain the confidence of the boy and facilitate the kidnap. The boy, in Abbas's eyes was beautiful but his desire for wealth and power overrode almost everything.

The last photo sent to the mother had shown the boy in a filthy djellaba sitting on the floor in a squalid little hovel his excrement fouling the floor in one corner and his urine running across most of the floor leaving him only a very small space to sit. There was no furniture in the shed and when the boy lay down to sleep part of his body was soaked in that urine.

Today, Michael was pulled from the hovel, stripped naked and taken to a bathroom in the palace. Abbas met him there. Michael fell into his arms and begged him to end the nightmare. He had no idea how long he had been in captivity, the days and nights just ran into one long period of degradation and terror. He was regularly pulled from the hovel and beaten. He had been fed properly for the last few days, but he was still much thinner than his old self and the bruising all over his body front and back was pretty awful. The filth had been constant, the smell so all-encompassing that he didn't notice it until he was pulled out and stripped in the fresh air of the grounds.

"Come, my little one we are going to bathe you and take you to the oasis for a swim, and we will sit and eat dates and fruit."

Michael thought he had been taken to Paradise, it was so long since he had been clean, and now he was able to wallow in fresh steaming hot water for as long as he liked. Abbas used sponges and sweet smelling soaps on him. Stood under a shower at the end of all the pampering, Michael asked Abbas if his ordeal was now over.

"Soon, little one, your father will pay the ransom and we can release you."

"I have not felt your soft lips round my penis for such a long time. Show me that you still love me by drinking my sperm once more."

The blowjob was not very good and Abbas realised how weak Michael was when he had to help him stand.

Michael could hardly believe it. He was given a clean white djellaba and Abbas held his hand as they walked down to the oasis. It was like a Garden of Eden, beautifully manicured lawns leading down to the water's edge. He was surprised to see so many people there, men, women and children. They were all sat around a cleared area that was covered with a plain brown rug. Abbas led Michael to it and they sat talking while a photographer ran a video recorder around them.

"We are going to record a message to send to your parents, so that they know you are well and will dispatch the ransom quickly now that all the negotiations are complete."

Michael smiled into the camera.

"Mum, and Dad, my friend tells me that you are ready to pay the ransom and I can come home. I am so pleased. Life here has been awful, but today Abbas has allowed me to bathe and I am ready to leave here. Please pay the ransom quickly."

The camera panned in to Abbas and he spoke.

"My uncle has decreed that Michael is to pay for the sins of his father. He is to be punished every day until the ransom is paid. I am sorry, I can do nothing about it."

Abbas walked off camera leaving Michael in the centre surrounded by watching women and children as four hefty guards moved in. Two of them took Michael's arms, pulled him to his feet and held them to his side. A third one approached and with no preamble took a knife from his belt, took hold of the neck of Michael's djellaba and slit it neck to floor. Michael looked into the camera showing total terror at this action. The remains of the djellaba was pushed off his shoulders by the guards holding his arms and allowed to fall to the floor. Michael was now stood naked as the camera panned in to take close ups of his genital area. He was turned round and the other two guards took a leg each and spread him very wide before he was forced to bend over and display his anus to the camera. In the sunlight the bruising on his body looked quite awful, Abbas came into the shot again.

"He has such a pretty little virgin hole. It is such a pity that we are not going to allow it to remain that way. Every day until we release him my uncle's personal guards are going to take their pleasure from it."

Michael wasn't a virgin by any means. Abbas had been only one of many lovers that Michael had taken before him, but he had not been sodomised since his kidnapping six months previously.

The camera swung then and ran along a line of ten men. They were all dressed in djellabas and didn't look anything special. The camera returned to Michael and showed him being laid on his back on the rug. His arms and legs were held apart so that he made a star shape. The camera once again showed his whole body. At a nod from Abbas, the legs were pulled further apart and bent up so that his knees were level with his shoulders and spread as wide. The camera zoomed in taking close-ups of his anus, running across his perineum to his testicles and finally his penis that had shrivelled up very small because of his fear.

To purchase the book, look for Finding Michael: Gay Suspense.

**Also by this Author:**

Mastered

Go For Goal Or... Guy?

Ruin

The Loser

Forced by the Military

Lucifer's Academy

So Full It Hurts!

Bully to Slave

Play & Pretend

The Submissive Bad Boy

Unexpected Island Mates

No Hoper

## From the Author

If you enjoyed any of my books then please share the love and click like on my books in Amazon.

If you write me a review and send me an email I will send you a free book, or many. (Just know that these emails are filtered by my publisher.)

Good news is always welcome.

One Last Thing, For Kindle Readers...

When you turn the page, Kindle will give you the opportunity to rate this book and share your thoughts on Facebook and Twitter. If you enjoyed my writings, would you please take a few seconds to let your friends know about it? Because... when they enjoy they will be grateful to you and so will I.

Thank You!

**Dexter Chase**
dexter_chase@awesomeauthors.org

# About the Author

Dexter Chase is a writer of hot, gay erotica stories in both paperback and Kindle versions.

His very first book published is **Mastered (Sensual Tales from Ancient Egypt)** which is about an eighteen-year old Ajax, who was taken as a slave and brought to a great house by a high-ranking soldier.

Check out his books and you'll enjoy extreme gay erotica of all time.